Vegan
Virgin
Valentine

Vegan
Virgin
Valentine

CAROLYN MACKLER

CANDLEWICK PRESS
CAMBRIDGE, MASSACHUSETTS

My warmest thanks to: My wonderful editors, Deborah Wayshak and Mara Bergman. Jodi Reamer, my agent and tireless champion. Everyone at Candlewick and Walker, for caring so much. Karen Bokram, my editor at *Girls' Life,* for whom I first discovered Mara Valentine. Dar Williams, who wrote the song "After All," which was an inspiration while I was working on this book. The village of Brockport for hosting this—purely fictional!— story. My stepsister, Michelle Seidman, who read the first four chapters and pointed me in the right direction. My parents, stepparents, parents-in-law, stepparents-in-law, and all those variations of siblings, for making me feel so loved. A special thanks to my grandmother, Betty Dalton, with whom I share a love of words and books.

And my deepest gratitude to my husband, Jonas Rideout—thank you for everything.

First paperback edition 2006

Library of Congress Cataloging-in-Publication Data is available.

Library of Congress Catalog Card Number 2004045774

ISBN 0-7636-2155-2 (hardcover)
ISBN 0-7636-2613-9 (paperback)

2 4 6 8 10 9 7 5 3

Printed in the United States of America

This book was typeset in Garamond.

Candlewick Press
2067 Massachusetts Avenue
Cambridge, Massachusetts 02140

visit us at www.candlewick.com

For my dear friend,
Jenny Greenberg,
with love

The first thing V did upon arriving

in Brockport was fool around with my ex-boyfriend. Well, not *the* first, but it happened within twenty-four hours of her plane landing at the Greater Rochester International Airport.

Her full name is Vivienne Vail Valentine, but she only answers to V.

My name is Mara Valentine. I'm seventeen and a senior in high school. I'll turn eighteen in late July, which makes me a Leo. Not that I know anything about astrology except my own sign. Anyway, it's a total joke because according to the *Democrat and Chronicle* horoscope page, the moon is heading into my house of romance this spring. Well, the only romance that ever entered my galaxy was Travis Hart. We were together spring of junior year. He definitely wanted more than my moon and he wanted it at the speed of light. He dumped me over Instant Messenger three days before the SATs. Thank God I still cracked fourteen hundred or I may have cracked his skull.

I'm a straight-A student and, yes, my parents both have that MY CHILD IS AN HONOR STUDENT bumper sticker on their cars. Those are now sharing fender space with the Yale bumper stickers they stuck on in December when I got accepted early admission.

Getting into Yale wasn't a total shocker. I've been in student government since junior high. Over the years, I've done pressure-cooker summer programs and Model UN and Odyssey of the Mind. I even got a part-time job at a café so my college application wouldn't make me look like a typical upper-middle-class brat who subsists solely on a hefty allowance.

My dad is a dentist with an office in Brockport. My mom does fundraising for the University of Rochester. I got my height from my dad. I'm a five-foot-ten vegan. I haven't touched dairy or meat or eggs in seven months, though sometimes I dream about grilled-cheese sand-wiches. I'm thin bordering on gangly with chin-length brown hair and hazel eyes. I have type A blood, a type A personality, and wear an A-cup bra.

My parents had me when they were in their forties. Now they're in their early sixties, which makes them ten or fifteen years older than most people's parents. Not that they show their age, aside from the fact that they gener-ally go to bed around sunset. We NEVER talk about sex, so I don't know the specifics of my eleventh-hour concep-tion. But I'm convinced that my parents brought me into this world to compensate for my older sister, Aimee, who was eighteen and skidding down a road to nowhere.

When I was still a baby, Aimee dropped out of college and moved to Vail, Colorado, to pursue her dream of becoming a ski instructor. Instead, she pursued a ski instructor and got pregnant by a guy she's only ever referred to as the Sperm Donor. V was born in September, by which time Aimee was living on a vineyard in California and pursuing her new dream of learning to make red wine.

By all logical deductions, V is my niece. But the whole aunt-and-niece-are-one-year-apart thing is too freaky to think about, so I basically try not to.

Aimee is now thirty-five and can't stick to one decision about her career, geographic location, or sexual partner. For the past six months, she's been living with a guy named Michael in San Diego and managing a Tex-Mex restaurant. Before that, she and Elias were tending an organic farm outside of Eugene, Oregon. Two years ago, it was bartending in New Orleans and an artists' commune in Vermont.

In between Aimee's transcontinental moves, she and V crash with us in Brockport for a few days. Aimee stays in the guest room upstairs. V sleeps on the air mattress on my floor. I dread these visits. If V and I weren't related, we'd never end up in the same stratosphere, much less the same bedroom. We're both tall and thin, but the similarities end there. V is one of those in-your-face girls. Besides, she acquires a new bad habit in every town. In Vermont, she lost her virginity to an eighteen-year-old harmonica player. She kept me up half the night describing their sexual encounters. In New Orleans, V honed her nymphomaniacal skills and added more guys to her list.

On the organic farm, of all places, she started smoking cigarettes. She burned through two packs while leaning out my window over the course of five nights.

My parents are always wringing their hands about Aimee and V. They long ago gave up on the idea of Aimee finishing college. Now they're just hoping she'll put down roots for more than a few months. But their pressing concern is V. They're frequently calling Aimee and offering to pay for V to take singing lessons or an SAT prep course. More than once, I've overheard my parents say things like, "V has so much unrealized potential. If only she lived with us, we could do wonders with her."

So that explains how much pressure is on me. Aimee has always been the Screwup. V, the Unrealized Potential. And me, the Only Hope.

But then, in January of my senior year, Aimee unloaded her daughter in Brockport. Less than a day later, V realized her potential with Travis Hart in the boys' locker room of my high school, which left me with only one hope: that V would get the hell out of my life.

❖ ❖ ❖

chapter one

My parents tag-teamed me on a blustery Monday evening in early January. It was flurrying like crazy out, one of those nights that practically guarantees school will be canceled the next day. Even so, I was sitting at my desk, studying for a quiz in psychology. My parents came into my room, stood on either side of me, and asked if we could have an impromptu Family Meeting.

Family Meetings are big in our household. We have Family Meetings to figure out where we're going for vacation. We had a Family Meeting when I said I didn't want to do Model UN senior year. When I was deciding where to apply to college, we had multiple Family Meetings to pore through books and read course catalogs before determining that Yale was the School for Me.

"What about?" I asked.

"Aimee called a few days ago," my dad said.

"She's moving to Costa Rica!" my mom exclaimed. "She wants to pursue her dream of cooking traditional Central American cuisine."

I glanced suspiciously at my mom's face, her crow's feet wrinkling, her smile lines cutting deep grooves. Usually when Aimee announces her latest dream, my mom gets all huffy about my older sister's flakiness. But this time around, she looked way too happy.

"So?" I asked. "Why the Family Meeting?"

My parents caught each other's eye for a second and then my dad said, "There are no English-language schools in the region where Aimee is going . . ."

"And V doesn't speak Spanish," my mom added.

My pulse sped up as I got a terrifying hunch about where this was headed. Sure enough, I was right. My parents proceeded to inform me that they'd already bought V a one-way plane ticket to western New York. She was going to arrive in a week and a half and stay in the guest room upstairs and continue her junior year at my high school.

I was so shaken, all I could think to say was, "Aimee wants to cook traditional Central American cuisine?"

My mom nodded. "Supposedly they use a lot of interesting spices."

"And so many variations on rice and beans," my dad said.

I stared out my window. The powdery snow was stick-

6

ing against the screen like confectioner's sugar in a metal strainer.

"The upside is that V is coming to live with us," my mom said. "Junior year is crucial. There's still time to get her on the college track."

"We've signed her up for an SAT prep course in Rochester," my dad said. "Aimee says V doesn't have her license yet, so Mom will drive her in on Tuesday evenings and I'll take her on Thursdays."

"Why didn't you tell me all this before?" I finally asked.

My parents glanced at each other. I knew exactly why they didn't tell me. They wanted everything signed and sealed before I could make any noise about it.

"We knew it would be an adjustment for you," my mom said.

"You and V have your differences," my dad said.

"But everything is going so well right now." I was thinking how I'd been planning to fast-forward through my five remaining months in Brockport. I've already applied to an academic program at Johns Hopkins this summer, where I can complete two college courses in eight weeks. My mind is on the future, anticipating a swift departure, no bumps or hurdles or nicotine-addicted nympho houseguests.

"It's going to be fine," my mom said.

My dad patted my shoulder. "You'll be so busy with your own things, you won't even notice V is here."

I stared up at my dad. Were we thinking about the same person?

"It's going to be fine," my mom said again.

Nine days later, we picked V up from the airport. Her honey-colored hair was long and her bangs hung like a Venetian blind over her eyes. My mom kept sweeping them toward V's temples, but they kept sliding back in place. Her nails, with chipped tangerine polish, were chewed all the way to the skin. There were freshly inked words on her left hand and fingers, but my parents were mauling her with hugs, so I couldn't make out what they said. And despite the fact that western New York in January is colder than Antarctica she was wearing a tank top, no bra, and jeans that were mutilated in the butt region.

When my dad went to retrieve the car from short-term parking, my mom took off her coat and insisted that V wear it. As V put on my mom's coat, I eyed the backpack she'd just slid off her bare shoulders. It was one of those hemp-cloth stoner satchels that made me wonder what new smoking habits she'd acquired in San Diego.

On the car ride back to Brockport, my parents asked about Aimee's newfound interest in Central American cuisine.

"Whatever," V said, rolling her eyes. "It's really about Campbell."

"Campbell?" my mom asked.

"Yeah," V said. "He's this surfer guy she met in

November. He's going to Costa Rica in search of killer waves. She's going to Costa Rica in search of killer orgasms."

We do not, I repeat, DO NOT talk about sex, much less orgasms, in the Valentine household.

My mom coughed. My dad swerved to the left, narrowly missing a Wegmans truck. No one said anything for a moment. V began gnawing at her fingernails. I stole a peek at her hand. Down each finger, from her pinkie to her pointer, she'd scrawled *fuck, fuck, fuck, fuck.* On her thumb it said *everyone.*

Yikes.

chapter two

After we got home from the airport, my dad carried V's duffel bags to the guest room and my mom heated up curry vegetables and basmati rice with lamb in a side dish for those of us who don't want our food coming in contact with flesh.

V helped herself to a heaping pile of lamb and a small haystack of rice.

"You don't like vegetables?" my dad asked.

V shook her head. "I'm all about baa-baa black sheep these days."

"It's lamb," I said.

As V ingested a chunk of meat, she began humming "Mary Had a Little Lamb."

She was totally doing it to piss me off. On the car ride home, my parents told her how I'm still a vegan. When she asked why anyone in their right mind would deprive themselves of hamburgers and pizza and ice cream, I said I'm grossed out by animal byproducts.

That's partially true. I've never been able to get over the fact that meat is essentially roadkill with pedigree or that eggs are unfertilized baby chickens. But I have my secret reasons, too. Basically, after Travis Hart broke up with me, I couldn't stop obsessing about him, about the rejection. Finally, after several hellish weeks, I decided I needed to obsess about something else. Something big. Which is why veganism made sense. It's all-consumingly obsessive. You have to read ingredients on every food item and bring peanut butter with you when you travel and only go to certain restaurants. It can be a total pain, but it helps keep my mind off things.

Toward the end of dinner, my parents asked V whether she was nervous to start at a new school.

"No big deal," V said. "This is the seventeenth school where I've been the new kid. It basically feels like . . . whatever."

"Seventeen?" My dad raised his thick eyebrows. "Is that really how many it's been?"

My mom's hands were clasped around her water glass like she was restraining herself from saying something less than nice about Aimee.

V nodded. "At some point, they all blend together. Same locker, different combination. Different lunchroom, same sour-milk stench. Same snobs, same moronic gossip."

My mom pushed V's bangs out of her eyes. Her fingers were damp from the glass perspiration, so this time V's hair slicked over to one side. V quickly looked down at her plate.

"Maybe Brockport will be different," my dad said. "After all, you know Mara. And I'm sure she can introduce you to people. She's involved in so many activities . . . I can't even keep track."

V and I caught each other's eye and had this quick I'm-sizing-you-up moment. I could tell by her smirk that she was thinking I'm a hand-raising, teacher-hugging goody-goody. But I didn't care because I'd already decided she was a class-ditching, chair-in-the-principal's-office-warming deadbeat.

"I have an idea!" my mom exclaimed. "Mara, why don't you grab a yearbook and we'll give V a quick who's who of Brockport High School."

I pushed my plate away from me. "Can't I just do the dishes? It's my night."

V smiled sweetly at my mom. "That's a great idea. It would make me feel *so* much better to look at a yearbook, you know, to see who's who."

"You're totally lying," I said. "You just said it doesn't matter, that we all blend together."

"*Lying* is a strong word," V said.

"You heard her," I said to my dad. "She said it doesn't matter who's who."

My mom and dad stared at each other like, *What now?*

My parents and I rarely fight. Sure, we disagree, but it's nothing that a few Family Meetings won't solve.

My dad ran his hands through his hair. It's mostly white and definitely in the Albert Einstein out-of-control subcategory. I inherited his hair texture, but I always blow-dry mine into submission.

"I'll take care of the dishes tonight," my dad finally said.

"Great," my mom said. "Mara, go grab your yearbook. Or do you want me to?"

I stabbed at my remaining piece of curried cauliflower. The tag team had just expanded from two to three.

My mom sat in the center of the couch with "Time of Our Lives" open on her lap. V and I sat on either side of her. "Time of Our Lives," by the way, is the name of last year's yearbook. I was the junior section editor but was attending a Model UN conference at Georgetown when they voted for the title. I think it's an idiotic name for a yearbook. If you give people the notion that high school is the time of their lives, won't it be depressing when they graduate and assume it's all downhill? But the yearbook adviser was also the person who was writing one of my college recommendation letters, so I wasn't about to argue it.

My mom was flipping through the pages, plunking her finger on various "nice kids," as she called them. Translation: they are college-bound with professional parents. It was strange to see my mom point out "Mara's friends."

Girls like Bethany Madison and Lindsey Breslawski. I ate lunch with them freshman, sophomore, and junior years, and we sometimes slept over at each other's houses.

We've grown apart this year. For all of senior year, I've been leaving the high school at eleven-forty. I'm in this special program for honor students called 3-1-3. The point is to take three years of high school, one year of high school and college together, and—if you get enough credits— three years of college. I'm in the "1" part now, so I have classes at SUNY Brockport every afternoon. Assuming I get accepted to the summer program at Johns Hopkins, I may be able to enter Yale as a second-year student.

All this to say that I don't eat lunch in the cafeteria anymore. I do the high-school thing in the morning, leave for the afternoon, and sometimes come back later for meetings. I still chat with Bethany and Lindsey in school, but we haven't talked on the phone or e-mailed in months.

My mom flipped through the "clubs" section and pointed out the myriad pictures of me. V kept making these snide little clucks. When my mom got to the Chemical-Free Fun Nights page and there I was— organizing Friday-night volleyball games as an alternative to killing brain cells—V actually snorted.

"Chemical-Free Fun Nights?" she asked. "What do you do? Give out chlorine and krypton at no cost? What fun!"

"Lay off," I said.

"I'm just teasing you, Mara. Chill out."

I hate when people tell me to chill out. It's just like

when I'm walking down the hall and some cheese-ball social-studies teacher bellows, "Smile, Mara!" like I'm supposed to be perennially pumped on Prozac.

I think my mom was sensing the tension. She flipped the page but unfortunately landed on a spread of candid shots from last year's Winter Ball. And smack dab in the center was that picture of me in a spaghetti-strap dress and Travis Hart in a suit, our arms around each other, with a caption that read *Valentine and Hart: 2-gether 4-ever.* My cohorts on the yearbook staff, confident that we were a match made in Hallmark heaven, slipped that in as a surprise. Surprise, all right. Travis tossed me aside in late April, by which time the yearbook was already at the printers. So when "Time of Our Lives" came out in June, I had to weather the public humiliation that Travis and I were no longer two and four, but one big zero. Not to mention that in the month since our split, he'd transformed into a male slut and was sleeping his way through the sophomore class.

"Valentine and Hart," V read in this singsong voice. "I didn't know you had a boyfriend. And *four*-ever, no less!"

"We're not together anymore," I said.

I could swear I heard my mom whimper. It's been more than eight months and my parents still haven't gotten over the fact that Travis and I didn't work out. It wasn't just the Valentine-Hart thing, though that was the icing on the cupcake. It's that on paper Travis is the Man for Me. He's over six feet, handsome, and my guy counterpart. Not the slut stuff, but on the overachieving front. We're in the same accelerated classes. We do most of the same extracurriculars. And we're currently in a heated competition for valedictorian of the senior class. With two marking periods to go, we're down to the decimal point. It's so insane because it won't even affect our academic futures. Three days after I got into Yale, Travis got accepted early decision to Princeton. But it's like whatever tension, sexual or otherwise, went on between us, we're now dueling it out on the GPA battlefield.

Sex, or lack of it, was our downfall. Travis treated our physical relationship with the cutthroat aggressiveness he applies to the rest of his life. It was all about conquests and scores. He was constantly pushing me to go further—second base, third base, that grand old slam. Early in our relationship, when he was trying to make it inside my bra and I kept shooing his hand away, he said, "What's the big deal? It's not like there's much there anyway."

Travis isn't a total jerk. He was just a jerky boyfriend. The brainiac circuit at my high school is small enough that I had to let go of my hostility toward him almost immediately. It's not like we're friends, but we're friendly enough. We're both on the senior-class council. We're cochairs of Chemical-Free Grad Night, which is this no-alcohol all-night party that the school throws the night of graduation. We're active in National Honor Society. We tutor sixth graders on Wednesday afternoons. Sometimes we even joke about our race for valedictorian, but I'm still determined to relegate him to salutatorian, to have the last and final laugh.

"How come you and the Hart guy didn't stay together forever?" V asked.

"We just didn't click," I said.

"What didn't you click about?"

I glanced at my mom.

"Maybe we shouldn't talk about this," my mom said.

"Why not?" V asked.

"Because it's over," I snapped. "Besides, it's not like he was anything to me. Just some guy."

"Very interesting," V said.

I reached over my mom and flipped the page.

Later that night, as I was flossing, V came into the bathroom and sat on the toilet lid.

"I can't believe Aimee has exiled me to fucking *Brockport*," she said.

I know I'm counting the seconds until I go away to college, but I was born and bred here, so I wasn't about to let V trash it. "What's so wrong with Brockport?"

"More like what's *right* with it? It's freezing cold. It's in the middle of nowhere. And what the fuck do you do for fun here?"

"It's not the middle of nowhere. Rochester is a half hour away."

V peered up at me through her long bangs. *"Rochester?* Are you kidding? Please tell me you're kidding."

I turned back to the mirror and slid the floss between two molars.

"So," V said, "it's interesting to see where things stand."

"Where things stand?"

"With your virginity."

I yanked the floss so hard it cut into my gums. "What are you talking about?"

"I'm talking about the fact that you're still a virgin. That you're going to turn eighteen in July and you still haven't done it."

I spat into the sink. There was blood in my saliva.

"Frankly," V said, "I'm worried about you."

"I don't need your concern," I said. "And, besides, you don't know anything about me. Unlike you, I choose to keep some things private."

"What's there to keep private? You didn't do it with that Hart guy."

"What makes you so sure?"

"I could tell by the way you talked about him," V said. "You did . . . let me guess. Second base? Maybe some haggling on his part to get to third. Oh, yeah. I bet you went down there once and got so freaked out that you vowed to never touch another dick for the rest of your life."

How did V know this? This is the kind of stuff I'd never tell *anyone* and here she was, banging the nail right on the head.

V was smiling. "I'm right, aren't I? I'm so right."

"Will you get out of here?"

V stood up and headed out of the bathroom, singing, "I'm so right. I'm so right. I'm *soooooooooo* right."

I slammed the door and locked it behind her.

chapter three

The next morning, I drove V over to the high school. We didn't say anything about the night before. Actually, we didn't say anything at all. I was silently raging at being trapped behind the slow-moving parade of buses that was turning the half-mile trip from my house into a hefty commute. And no matter how many times I adjusted the defroster, I couldn't get the windshield to stop fogging.

V stared out her window at the icy soccer fields. She was wearing an oversize army-navy jacket and flicking a convenience-store lighter on and off. That was annoying me, too, but I didn't feel like telling her to quit it and risk getting her started about something.

We didn't make it into the school until the first bell had already rung. I walked V to the main office and introduced her to Rosemary, the administrative assistant. I'm frequently in the main office meeting with Mr. Bonavoglia.

Otherwise known as Mr. B. He's the vice principal, in charge of all student affairs.

"Vivienne Vail Valentine," Rosemary chirped. She has curling-iron-shaped bangs and an unflappably sunny demeanor. "Your records got faxed over from California yesterday. With Mara's reputation here, we are thrilled to have another Valentine at Brockport High School. And you're both so tall! Do you play basketball?"

People are always asking me that, too. Just like how everyone always asks whether I'm a real heartbreaker because my last name is Valentine. I hate both of those questions. To set the record straight, the answers are No and Most Definitely Not.

"Just call me V," V said. Her hands were rammed in the pockets of her jacket. As we were driving over to school, I noticed that the *fucks* on her fingers had faded since yesterday.

"V," Rosemary repeated. "I'll try to remember that. So remind me . . . how are you girls related?"

"V is my . . ." I paused.

"I'm her niece," V said.

"Niece?"

"I have a sister who's almost twenty years older than me," I said quickly. "She's V's mom."

"A sister by the same parents?"

Why are people so darn nosy? The obvious subtext to this is *Your parents were still doing it two decades later?* Gross.

V was opening her mouth to say something when the second bell rang.

"Almost time for announcements!" Rosemary exclaimed. "Let me go look for your records, Vivi . . . I mean, V."

Rosemary headed into an adjacent room. V picked up a cafeteria menu and began fanning her neck. "Principals' offices make me sweat my ass off," she said.

I glanced around to make sure no one had heard her. V unzipped her army-navy jacket, wriggled out of it, and hung it over one arm.

Oh my God.

No wonder V had come down to the kitchen this morning already wearing her jacket. Underneath, she had on a hot-pink tank top with silver lettering that said I'M JUST A GIRL WHO CAIN'T SAY NO. To make matters worse, she was braless yet again and her you-know-whats were poking through her shirt, feeling the morning chill.

"What's up with that tank top?" I hissed.

"What do you mean?"

"Don't you think that's making the wrong first impression?"

"What first impression do you think I want to make?"

I shifted my bag around on my shoulder and glanced up at the clock. Three minutes until homeroom.

Ms. Green walked into the office. She's one of the younger teachers at the high school. She teaches sophomore English but also directs the school plays, so she's frequently trailed by aspiring thespians hoping to brown-nose their way into a leading role.

Ms. Green waved at me and then eyed V. "Are you new here?"

"I'm Mara's niece," V said.

I flinched. Why couldn't V just be my cousin? My *long-distance* cousin.

But all Ms. Green said was, "Cool shirt. Like Ado Annie."

V smiled. "You know Ado Annie?"

"Of course." Ms. Green walked over to the mail cubbies and pulled out a few envelopes.

I had no idea what they were talking about and I didn't want to be late for homeroom, so I tapped my fingers on the counter. "I've got to run," I said. "Rosemary will send you over to the guidance counselors to get your schedule figured out. Is that okay?"

V chewed at her thumbnail. "I *cain't* say no."

I didn't see V for the rest of the day. I left school before noon, headed over to the college for my Tuesday/Thursday statistics class, ate a Boulder Bar, and spent the afternoon holed up in Drake Memorial Library. I was busy memorizing influential Supreme Court rulings for a test in government the next day when my cell phone vibrated on the table.

I glanced at the caller ID. My dad. My parents and I

have a Family Talk plan where all our cell phones are linked so it's free minutes whenever we call each other. They keep frequent tabs on my whereabouts, but it's not like I'm doing anything shady, so I don't really mind.

I pressed the "answer" button and said hello.

"Mara?" my dad asked. He always does that, asks if it's me when he knows for a fact it's me because he dialed my number. "Where are you?"

"I'm in the college library," I said in a hushed voice. "I can't really talk."

"Oh, okay," my dad said. "I just got back from Wegmans, and Mom is on her way from work. Will you be home soon?"

"What time is it?"

"Six-twenty."

I was working at Common Grounds that night, but I didn't have to be there until seven-thirty. It's a five-minute drive from the college to my house, so I could easily pull off the family dinner. But I just didn't feel like seeing V. Besides, the government test was going to count for 15 percent of my grade and, at this point, I'm striving for any edge over Travis.

"I'm going to keep studying. I'll head to work from here."

"What will you do for dinner?"

"I'll grab something at Mythos," I said, referring to this vegan-friendly Greek place right across the street from Common Grounds.

"Do you have enough money on you?"

"Yeah."

"It's already dark out. Will you be careful when you walk to your car?"

"I know, I know, I will."

"Okay, sweetie. Have fun tonight. Mom and I will probably be asleep when you get home, but we'll leave the yard lights on."

It was great to be at Common Grounds. We were crammed with customers all evening. College students hunched over mugs of chai, writing in their journals. Local burnouts doing espresso shots in between playing Hacky Sack under a street lamp on the snowy sidewalk. Middle-aged types consuming the mother of paradoxical desserts: a nonfat decaf latte and fudge cake. My favorites, however, were the Internet daters.

Claudia and I have a field day with them. Claudia Johns is a junior at SUNY Brockport. We do all our shifts together, so over the past year we've honed the art of identifying dot-com matches.

"Twenty-something mama's boy seeks, well, mom," Claudia recently said when a geeky guy held the door for a chubby woman who looked like she was at least ten years older than him.

I responded with, "I like walking on sandy beaches, eating candlelit dinners, and having someone read *The Runaway Bunny* to me at bedtime."

Claudia giggled. "And what do you think is the woman's deal?"

I thought for a second before saying, "She just wants a bling-bling on her fing-fing before her biological clock goes ding-ding."

Claudia and I were in hysterics over that one. We didn't sober up until James, our boss, got on our case for making fun of customers. "Just have a little discretion," he said. "We still need to sell them an overpriced cup of coffee."

It's weird to call James our boss. He's more like a friend. James McCloskey is twenty-two and the owner of Common Grounds. He opened the café when he was only nineteen. I'm constantly telling him he's totally prodigal. Especially since it's not a grungy dive. It's dimly lit, with an exposed brick wall, an assortment of hand-painted tables, and a fully functional vintage coffee roaster.

I've never been sure why James didn't go to college. He's one of the smartest people I've ever met. He and I are always debating things like What Constitutes Art and Does Advertising Influence Us Even Though We Swear It Doesn't. He has this ability to think it over and form his own opinions, not just read and regurgitate an article, like I always seem to do.

That Thursday night, Claudia arrived at work shaken up because an eighty-year-old guy nearly plowed her down as she was crossing Holley Street. This prompted James and me into a big debate about whether senior citizens should automatically get their licenses taken away. I was sitting on the stool behind the counter. I'm taller than both Claudia and James, so I usually sit down when I'm talking to them. I was saying things like, "Grandma and Grandpa are a hazard to themselves and everyone else on the road, not to mention that they drive in first gear on the highway." James kept insisting that many elderly people are fine drivers and the DMV should just do a yearly evaluation of their abilities.

After ten minutes, Claudia began grinding coffee beans so loudly that neither of us could talk. "Will you two quit it already?" she shouted. "*I'm* the one who almost died tonight, not you guys."

I cracked up. That's exactly what I love about Common Grounds. It gets me out of myself. I took the job here to diversify my college application, but it's become so much more. When I'm serving coffee and goofing around with Claudia and James, I feel like a different person. I'm not obsessing about my grade-point average or hyperanalyzing a conversation or thinking about my to-do list for the upcoming week, month, and year.

Around nine-thirty, James was tinkering with the coffee roaster at the back of the café. Claudia was brewing a pot of Mocha Java. Just as I squirted cleanser on the counter and began scrubbing off a coffee stain, a beefy middle-aged guy strutted through the door. He was wearing a black leather jacket and had this pimpish gold earring in his left lobe. Several steps behind him was a tiny blond woman, probably in her early thirties. Her hands fluttered in front of her face, as if she were hoping no one would recognize her.

"Recent divorcé paid a visit to Piercing Pagoda before getting 'out there' again," I whispered to Claudia as I tossed a paper towel in the trash.

As Claudia glanced in their direction, I noticed that her licorice-black hair was pulled into a messy ponytail. That's odd for Claudia. She's one of those lucky souls with straight lustery hair. She's always running to the bathroom with a brush in hand and then shaking her mane around her shoulders.

"And the girl?" I asked. "What's the blond girl's deal?"

"The blond girl . . . the blond girl . . ." Claudia stared at them like she was trying to come up with a response. Finally she moaned and said, "I'm sorry. I'm really pining tonight. I can hardly think straight."

"You are?"

Claudia nodded sadly.

"Oh, Claud," I said. "Are you going to tell him soon?"

Claudia shrugged. "I don't know. I've dropped enough hints, haven't I? If he hasn't guessed by now, he must not like me back."

Claudia was talking about James. That's the Big Unspoken Dynamic at Common Grounds. Claudia is in love with James. She's had a crush on him since we both started here last year. She's always giggling at everything he says and complimenting his sweaters and bringing him cans of chicken soup when he's got the slightest sniffle. He's definitely nice to her. But he's nice to everyone, so I've never been able to figure out whether he likes her back.

James is three inches shorter than me, which makes him a perfect match for Claudia. He's got broad shoulders, a cute smile, and medium-length chestnut hair that he usually keeps in a ponytail. Claudia says it flatters his bone structure, but I just can't get into male ponytails.

The guy with the leather jacket and the blond woman approached the counter. I glanced briefly at James. He was still over by the roaster. I could have sworn he was watching me because we made eye contact for a second. As he looked away, I felt this weird thump in my stomach.

Claudia poured coffee for the customers. I rang them up on the cash register.

Once they headed to the condiment island, I turned to Claudia and said, "Beautiful black-haired Common Grounds employee finally works up the nerve to tell the guy she loves how she feels about him . . ."

Claudia whimpered. "And loses her job and her pride in the process?"

"That wasn't what I was going to say."

"Then what?"

"Maybe, just maybe, he loves her back."

"Do you really think that could happen?"

"You won't know unless you try."

"Thanks, Mara," Claudia said as she dried her hands on a dishcloth. "I really needed to hear that."

chapter four

When Ash Robinson approached my locker the next morning, I knew something was up. Ash is the school gossip. The only times she ever seeks me out is when she either has dirt or wants dirt. When Travis dumped me last April, she sent me an e-mail inviting me to the Strand with her. From the ticket counter to the concession stand, she had questions. "Was it another girl? Are you devastated? Pissed?" I was finally off the hook when the lights dimmed. By then Ash was craning her neck around the theater, scanning for faces from school.

"Hey, Mara." Ash leaned against the locker next to mine.

"Hey, Ash." I closed my government notebook. The end-of-the-unit test was first period, so I'd been doing some last-minute cramming. "What's up?"

"I just wanted to know if you'd heard. I didn't want you to find out from, like, the wrong person."

Bingo.

"Heard what?"

"About your . . . uh . . . What is she again? That V girl?"

"Long story, but I have a sister who's much—"

"Right," Ash said. "About her and Travis Hart."

"What did you say?"

"About V and Travis. How they"—Ash leaned in so close I could smell the Dentyne Ice on her breath—"fooled around yesterday."

I felt like I'd had the wind knocked out of me. My heart started racing as Ash told me how Travis and V wound up in the same fourth-period gym class. Ash wasn't there, but she heard from highly reliable sources that V didn't have any gym clothes, so she had to sit in the bleachers and dodge flyaway birdies. After a few minutes, Travis abandoned his badminton partner and became V's one-man welcome committee. Travis is senior class president, so he can pretty much get away with murder. I'm senior class treasurer, so the most I can get away with is borrowing a dollar if I'm short on cash in the cafeteria. Not that I eat school food, but that's beside the point.

No one is sure whether Travis knew up front that V was my relative, but someone heard him laughing and saying, "*Cain't say no,* huh?" Someone else saw her stroking his head where his hair was recently buzzed. And the next time that person looked up, Travis and V had disappeared. Toward the end of the period, Ted Papazian went into the boys' locker room. He heard murmuring in the shower area and, upon glancing into a stall, witnessed Travis going at it with a tall, longhaired girl wearing a pink tank top.

By this point, Ash's eyes were bulging out of their sockets. "Lips locked," Ash said. "Hands everywhere. Full-frontal grinding."

"Did Ted say anything to them?"

"No, he got out of there fast. He didn't want to be, like, a pervert."

"Did anyone ask Travis about it later?"

Ash shook her head. "He left for his college class right after gym, so no one saw him for the rest of the day."

"Do you think they . . . ?"

She shrugged. "I'm just stating the facts. I'm not jumping to any conclusions."

The first bell rang. People started slamming their lockers and filtering into homerooms. My throat felt tight, like I was going to cry. I took a few shallow breaths.

"I'm so sorry, Mara," Ash said, patting my arm. "I could hardly believe it myself. There's, like, no family loyalty these days, you know?"

I hugged my notebook to my chest and began crying. Ash reached into her purse, pulled out a minipack of Kleenex, and handed me a tissue. She'd obviously come prepared.

• • •

32

I spent all of homeroom fending off tears. First period was even worse. I couldn't concentrate during the government test and kept mixing up the Supreme Court rulings and completely blanked on which state had the ballot controversy during the Bush-Gore presidential election. It didn't help that Travis was three seats up, his spiky head hunched over his paper. I kept thinking about what Ash said. *Lips locked. Hands everywhere. Full-frontal grinding. Lips locked. Hands everywhere. Full-frontal grinding. Lips locked. Hands everywhere. Full-frontal grinding.*

As soon as the bell rang, I handed in my test and bolted out of the classroom, hoping Travis wouldn't follow me. Ever since ninth grade, we've been comparing notes after anything from a pop quiz to a final exam. I know exactly what he got on the SATs. He knows that on the English Regents, I made the mistake of spelling *fervor* with a *u* instead of an *e* but compensated by kicking butt on the essay questions. It's sort of unhealthy the way we've played into each other's grade obsession, but it's gotten us into Princeton and Yale so I guess I'm not complaining.

Travis grinned as he caught up with me. "I was stumped by the second question, but then it hit me. *Brown versus Board of Education.* From there, I cruised through. What about you?"

I shook my head. I was barely even thinking about the fact that—damn it!—I mistakenly wrote *Wade v. Board of Education.* I was more wondering if Travis is a clueless idiot. Does he think I don't know? And let's say I *didn't* know, how could he full-frontal grind with V one day and act totally normal with me the next?

"Are you okay, Valentine?" Travis asked. "Did you screw it up or something?"

I started walking faster.

"You *did* screw it up!" Travis said, keeping up with me. "So sweet! My GPA just left yours in the dust, didn't I? I can *taste* my valedictory speech. *Mmmm, mmmmm —*"

I whipped my face toward Travis. "Will you shut up already?"

"I'm just kidding. You know how we always—"

"Didn't you hear me? I don't want to talk right now."

"What's your deal? Are you PMS-ing?"

I clenched my fists. "You don't *know* what my deal is?"

Travis shook his head.

"Get a freaking conscience," I snapped.

And then I took off in the other direction, down a stairwell, and through the English hallway. I didn't stop until I was certain I'd left Travis far behind.

I was still fuming after fourth period. I headed home, ate a peanut butter sandwich without even tasting it, and went into my room to check my e-mail.

Ash had sent me a text message from her cell phone saying to call or e-mail if I want to talk. *As if,* I thought, deleting it. I deleted about fourteen e-mails enticing me to buy Viagra and refinance my home. Then I saw an e-mail from Bethany Madison. It looked like she'd sent it about fifteen minutes ago.

Mara—
Hey there. It's been awhile . . . Hope your address is still the same. Ash said you were upset this morning. Leave it to Ash to spill the beans, right? Lindsey was in that gym class, so she confirmed those beans, in case you were wondering. Travis sucks, and you can tell him I said that! You can always call me if you want to talk. It's been so long. Almost feels like you've already left for Yale.
Bethany

I was about to reply to Bethany when an IM from TravisRox188 popped up on my screen.

Yo, Valentine. R u there?

What do u want? I pounded on the keys as I typed.

Over at the college. About to go to class. Still searching for my freaking conscience . . .

U really don't know?

If I did, would I ask u? ;)

I forgot how Travis always did those annoying winky emoticons. I felt pissed just looking at it.

Does the 22nd letter of the alphabet mean anything to u? I wrote.

He didn't respond for a second. I pictured him sitting there, counting on his fingers, so I quickly wrote, *V, u remedial idiot.*

U mean your . . . What is she again?

Not about to give u my family tree, but u totally should have stayed away.

What can I say? Travis wrote back. *I like tall girls whose last name is Valentine. ;) ;) ;)*

That's SICK and INCESTUOUS!!! I typed.

For your info, what . . . or who . . . I do is NOT your business. We broke up almost a year ago, in case u forgot.

Ouch. I bit down on my tongue and wrote, *U can do whatever the hell u want, but there r some boundaries, u know? Things u shouldn't do EVER.*

Travis didn't respond for a moment. I was about to log off when one sentence popped up.

I can see u haven't changed.

I was tempted to hurl my stapler through the monitor, but instead I grabbed my keys and cell phone and stomped out to my car. If I was determined to beat Travis for valedictorian before, now I wanted to kick his salutatorian butt all the way to Princeton, New Jersey.

As far as V, I was too pissed to even think about her.

I was still angry when I got to the college for my improv dance class. Not a good idea. Even when I'm feeling fine, I hate this class. I wish I'd never registered for it, but SUNY Brockport has a renowned dance program, so I figured I should cash in while I had the opportunity. Big mistake.

The teacher is Dr. Hendrick. He used to be in the chorus of a Broadway musical several decades ago, so he still thinks he's hot stuff. The only hot thing about him is that he sweats like an ice cube on a summer day.

We've had four classes so far this semester, during which he's spent the entire fifty minutes calling out things like, "Be a pine tree!" "Be somber!" "Be a baby bird!" A guy pounds on drums in the corner, and all the students sway and mope and tweet accordingly.

Today was more of the same. We'd just finished our stretches when Dr. Hendrick shouted, "Be a gazelle running through the wilds of Africa!"

The drummer pounded a steady rhythm. Everyone started springing around the room, chests forward, feet flying. I slunk after them, looking more like a deer in the woods. *After* it's been shot. Maybe I'm uptight, but I just can't get into the whole hippie-dippy-let-loose thing.

Dr. Hendrick trotted after us, his forehead glistening. "Be popcorn sizzling on hot oil!"

Everyone flung their bodies around. I shook my arms a little. I glanced in the mirror. I looked like I was having a seizure.

"Now close your eyes and move like you do when you're happy. Do happy, however you interpret that."

I shut my eyes. The drummer began a frenetic rhythm. I stood still for a few seconds before peeking. The whole class was swaying and bouncing and twirling. Even Dr. Hendrick was galloping around, his eyelids scrunched shut, sweat drenching his underarms.

Then he opened his eyes and I was busted.

"Ms. Valentine, why aren't you doing happy?"

As my classmates jiggled and the drummer pounded, I stared at Dr. Hendrick. *Doing happy?* Today of all days, I'm supposed to be *doing happy?* Besides, I'm just not the happy sort of person. Sure, I feel good when I get an A or when someone compliments me on what I'm wearing, but if you're looking for Mary Poppins or the von Trapp family, you're not going to find that in me.

Dr. Hendrick and I stared each other down for a moment, and then he shouted to the class, "Stop doing happy and start being radishes. Not Saran-wrapped and miserable in the grocery store, but radishes in a garden. A lush, fertile garden full of radishes."

This guy was definitely a freak.

When I got home, V was in the kitchen, swigging directly from the carton of milk.

"Stop it," I said. "That's disgusting."

She gulped for a few more seconds before smiling at me, a white mustache spreading across her upper lip. "What do you care? It's not like you even drink milk."

"I care because it's unsanitary." I unlaced my boots and set them in the laundry room. "Besides, if you do it with the milk, you're probably doing it with the orange juice and the lemonade."

"Yeah, I'm a real refrigerator slut," V said.

"Take out the 'refrigerator' part and you're right on target."

V reached into the cupboard and pulled out the Oreos. She split one apart and scraped off the filling with her teeth. "What are you talking about?"

"I'm talking about Travis Hart."

"So that's his first name?" V sat on one of the stools. "I couldn't remember."

I felt like I'd been punched in the gut. "So it's true?" I asked, furiously. "You and Travis . . . in the locker room yesterday?"

V split another Oreo in half and scraped out the filling. She wasn't eating the brown cookie part, just licking them clean and lining them in a row on the cutting board.

"You knew I was with him last year," I said, anger building in my throat. "How could you do that?"

"You said he was nothing to you."

"That doesn't make it okay," I snapped.

V didn't say anything as she licked all of the cookies another time and then piled them in a stack.

"I can't believe you stole away *my* ex-boyfriend on your first day at *my* school."

"*Ex* is the operative word here," V said, laughing sarcastically. "He didn't exactly belong to you."

I raced toward her, seriously feeling like I was going to kick her. But, instead, I kicked over the other stool. As it crashed to the floor, I ran into my bedroom and slammed the door.

• • •

I stayed in my room for almost thirty minutes. I arranged all my papers so they were in two neat piles. I put my pens and markers in the plastic student government cup that I got at a leadership conference two summers ago. I straightened my closet, hanging all my clothes in the same direction and making sure my shoes were paired up and relocating any sweaters that drifted into the shirt section.

I kept thinking about all the things I wished I'd said to V. About how there's a right and wrong in this world and what she did is definitely in the wrong category. About how you can't let hormonal urges come before friends and even family. About how she betrayed me by fooling around with Travis and I'll never forgive her for that.

Once it was all clear in my head, I went into the living room to give her an earful, but she wasn't there or in the kitchen. I opened the door to the stairwell leading to the guest room. As I headed upstairs, I smelled something sort of smoky and sweet and peppery.

It was pot. *Oh my God.* V was getting high up there.

I've only been around people smoking pot one time, but it's such a distinctive smell, I could place it anywhere. It was at that Model UN conference at Georgetown. We all stayed in the dorms and, ironically, it was the kids representing the Netherlands who brought the joint. A few of my teammates smoked, but I didn't try it. It wasn't just that I was president of Chemical-Free Fun Nights, though that wouldn't have looked very good if it got around. It's more that I didn't like the idea of losing control, of having a surge of unwelcome emotion, of giggling at stupid things and crying at nothing, like the girl representing Iceland was doing.

I stood on the landing for a second, breathing in another whiff. So I was right about V and the new bad habit she'd acquired in San Diego. Her stoner backpack had definitely made me wonder.

As I turned and stomped back down the stairs, V cracked open her door and shouted, "I'll kill you if you tell G-ma and G-pa."

"I'm so scared," I said.

V slammed her door and I slammed the door to the stairwell, and suddenly I realized that in the past forty-eight hours, I've slammed more doors than I've probably slammed in the previous year.

chapter five

V and I barely spoke over the weekend. She was out with my parents a lot. When she was home, I was either working at Common Grounds or studying at the college library or going for long walks in the frostbit January weather, just to be off her radar screen.

Monday was Martin Luther King Day, so the high school and the college were closed, but my parents were going to work. When I woke around nine, they were already gone. V was still sleeping, so I wolfed down a banana and a bowl of cereal with soymilk. Then I bundled up in jeans, a long undershirt, a sweater, two pairs of socks, boots, a hat, a scarf, gloves, and my coat. I put my cell phone in the coat pocket and headed outside.

The sky was clear blue and the air was freezing. I walked across town to the canal. I took a right on the towpath and hiked almost all the way to Adam's Basin. I only saw one person along the way, a middle-aged woman with a golden retriever. We waved at each other. I was relieved she didn't try to chat with me because I wasn't in the mood for small talk.

My cell phone rang. I dug it out of my pocket, glanced at the caller ID, and stabbed the "answer" button with my gloved finger.

"Hey, Mom."

"Where are you, sweetie? Dad talked to V a few minutes ago and she said you weren't there when she got up. Are you at the college library?"

"I'm walking on the canal."

"You're *what*? Did you say you're walking down the canal?"

"Yeah."

"Sweetie, it's ten below out with the wind-chill factor. Are you okay? Is everything okay?"

"I'm fine."

"Want Dad to come pick you up? I'm sure he can leave his office for a few minutes."

"No," I said. "I want to walk."

On my way back to Brockport, there was a fierce blast whipping into my face. One of those insanely frigid winds off Lake Ontario. My eyes and nose were watering. My cheeks were tingling. My fingers ached. And my thighs were frozen solid.

Unfortunately, however, my brain wasn't numb.

I couldn't stop obsessing about how Travis and V had hooked up. And what Travis had said in the IM, about how I haven't changed. And the agonizing fact that V was living with us indefinitely. There was only so long I could avoid my own house.

That night, my parents had dinner with friends in Rochester. V was watching television. I was in my room eating dried apple slices and attempting to calculate estimates for my statistics class, but she had the volume on so high I couldn't focus. It was some stupid sitcom and the laugh track was giving me a headache.

After several earsplitting guffaws, I stormed into the living room, grabbed the remote control off the coffee table, and lowered the volume.

"Why'd you do that?" V asked.

"Are you deaf or something?"

"Come on," V said as she bit off a chunk of some beef-jerky–looking brown thing. "It's funnier that way."

I didn't even respond. Still holding the remote control, I returned to my room. I knew I was being a bitch, but V had asked for it.

V followed me in and stood in my doorway. "Why are you being such a bitch?"

I sat at my desk and stared down at *Elementary Statistics*.

"It's Travis, isn't it? You're still pissed about that."

I clenched my jaw.

"You said it wasn't anything," V said as she chewed at her nails.

"What wasn't anything?"

"You and Travis. You said you guys were nothing, so I

figured . . . We were just having fun. Don't you ever have fun?"

"You're unbelievable," I said. "You're turning this around and making it about *me?*"

"I'm just saying you should lighten up."

"At other people's expense?"

"God," V said. "You sure are wound tight."

I'd had it. I'd really had it.

"Will you get out of my room?"

"Don't get so offended. I'm just saying—"

I chucked the remote control at V. She dodged it, so it smacked against the wall and split open.

"I didn't know you had a violent side!" V shouted, scurrying down the hallway.

As I watched the batteries roll across the hardwood floor, I couldn't believe my peaceful existence had come to this.

To make matters worse, my parents were doting on V. On Tuesday, they both took off the afternoon so they could bring her to the mall and buy her a new wardrobe. They rationalized it by saying that she didn't have any clothes suitable for an East Coast winter, which explained the sweaters, jacket, boots, and olive-colored scarf. *All fine and great,* I thought, *but please explain the funky black pants and four cute shirts and expensive skin cream.*

When I commented about this to my dad, he said he was surprised at my attitude. He told me how I've never been denied anything and V has had it hard and they're just trying to make up for lost time with her. By the way he talked, you'd have thought V was Cinderella and I was a wicked stepsister. If only he knew that V had hooked up with my Prince Not-So-Charming and was getting high on something other than life on the second floor of the palace.

V definitely played up the lovable act with my parents. Whenever they were around, she was all smiles and sweetness, snuggling into the crook of my dad's arm and combing his wild white hair with her fingers. When my mom complained of a backache, she helped with the laundry and the dishes. She even carried two loads of firewood up from the basement. But as soon as my parents were out of sight, V instantly reverted back to V. She was loud and obnoxious. She chugged directly from the carton. Once she picked a booger out of her nose, rolled it between her thumb and pointer finger, and flicked it across the room. Plus, she was constantly watching me, quick to point out any and all character flaws. It was driving me insane.

On Wednesday afternoon, when I got home from my weekly volunteer gig of tutoring sixth graders, I found a thick envelope in the mailbox. It was from Johns Hopkins, telling me I was accepted to their precollege summer program. I speed-dialed my mom's cell phone as I walked through the side door. V was conked out on the couch, watching TV. The volume wasn't deafening, so I sat on the comfy chair and told my mom the news. Ten seconds after we hung up, my dad called my cell. My mom had told him and he wanted to say congrats. Just after we said goodbye, I called him back to ask if he could bring home takeout from Mythos tonight. While we were discussing what to get, my mom beeped in on the other line and shouted, "HOLY MOLY! With two more college courses this summer, my baby could enter Yale as a SECOND-YEAR STUDENT in the fall!"

I was like, "Yeah! Yay! I know!"

I pushed the "hang up" button and set my phone on the armrest. That's when I noticed that V was staring at me through her long bangs.

"Freaky," she said.

I sighed. "What now?"

"How you and your parents are with your cell phones. It's like you've got a satellite umbilical cord to them."

"We do not! I was just calling them with good news. Don't go looking for things that aren't there."

"It's time to cut the cord," V said.

"Don't say that."

With one hand, V pantomimed an umbilical cord extending out from her bellybutton. With her other hand posing as a butcher knife, she hacked through it. The whole time, she was chanting, "Cut the cord, cut the cord, cut the cord."

The following night, I was in the kitchen making vegetarian chili when V sauntered in.

"Putting beef in there?" she asked.

I continued dicing up the pepper. "I bet you can guess the answer to that."

"What's up with your whole vegan thing anyway?"

"It's not my *whole vegan thing.* I'm just a vegan. It's no big deal."

"But *why?* Aren't you denying yourself all the pleasures in life?"

"There are lots of good things to eat without having to consume dead animals," I said. I obviously wasn't about to tell her my Secret Travis Reason, so instead I said, "Did you know that by leading a meat-free life, you can save nearly eight hundred chickens, five cows, and twenty pigs?"

V laughed. "I'll probably eat more like *ten* cows in my lifetime."

I concentrated on cutting the pepper, careful to make all the pieces a uniform size.

"That doesn't explain why you don't eat eggs and dairy," V said.

I turned up the flame on the frying pan and gathered together the peppers and onions and minced garlic. "I just don't like to eat anything that comes out of a cow's udder or a chicken's butt," I said.

"Eggs don't come out of the chicken's butt," V said. "They come out of a chicken's—"

"I know!" I tossed the vegetables into the frying pan.

I'd turned it up too high, so the olive oil spat all over the place. I lifted the pan off the flame and dodged the crackling tears of oil.

"Why can't you say that word?" V asked.

"What word?"

"*Vagina.* That's where the eggs come from. A chicken's vagina."

A chicken's vagina. My God. V is too much.

"Will you leave me alone?" I said, sighing heavily. "I'm going to screw up the chili."

"Just say the word and I'll vanish." V snapped her fingers. "Just like that."

"I don't want to," I said, growing increasingly frustrated. It wasn't just that I didn't *want* to say it. It was that I couldn't say it. Same goes for the P-word. The thought of saying them out loud makes me feel totally icky.

V opened the fridge and got out the bottle of ketchup. Raising it to her mouth like a microphone, she began singing, *"On top of va-giiiiii-na, all covered with snow. I lost my va-giiiiii-na, from courting too —"*

Just then my dad rapped on the back door. V halted midnote and ran over to let him in, a huge smile on her face.

"Hey, girls!" he said, stomping his boots on the mat. "What do you look so happy about?"

I glanced at V. She winked at me and then said, "Mara and I were just making dinner and talking about va—"

"Vegans," I said, cutting her off. "We're talking about why I'm a vegan."

My dad inhaled through his nose. "Smells great," he said. "I'm so glad to see you're cooking together."

"V isn't exactly helping me."

"I'm keeping you company," V said, sticking out her bottom lip. "Doesn't that count for anything?"

"It counts for a lot," my dad said as he wrapped his arms around V and kissed the top of her head.

"Thanks for saying that, G-pa," V said.

"Anytime, sweetie."

I pushed my wilting vegetables around with a wooden spoon, feeling pissed at V and my dad and the world in general.

On the school front, things were shaky, too. I bombed last Friday's government test. Not bombed, but I got an 84 percent, which would definitely set me back a decimal point or so in the race for valedictorian. When the teacher handed us our tests, I stared down at my desk, willing myself not to look up in case Travis turned around and mouthed his score to me.

Travis and I still hadn't spoken since we'd IM-ed last week. I'd consulted with Ash Robinson, and she'd said that V and Travis—to the best of her knowledge—were a one-period stand. Ash mentioned that V had been eating lunch with Brandon Parker, our friendly high-school marijuana dealer. He's nineteen, has a peach-fuzz mustache, and should have graduated two years ago but keeps getting suspended for smoking pot on school premises. Ash also told me she'd heard from a reliable source that Travis had been spotted with a girl from the neighboring village of Holley over the long weekend.

"Big boobs, big hair, and a big reputation for being easy" was how Ash put it.

"I hope she has a *biiig* case of herpes, too," I said.

"Mara?" Ash giggled nervously. "You sound bitter. Are you bitter?"

I shook my head. "Just ignore me, okay?"

But the Travis thing was definitely getting to me. Whenever I saw his face, I pictured him grinding with V in a shower stall. It felt like a throwback to the weeks after he dumped me, when the sight of him or the sound of his voice was enough to start me crying.

It didn't help that I saw him after school on Tuesday at the National Honor Society meeting, where he solicited a hug from every girl except me. And after school on Wednesday, as he was also tutoring sixth graders. And before school on Thursday, at the monthly hot-chocolate-and-bagels student government gathering. He stood up and made an announcement about how the senior class is doing a candygram fundraiser on Valentine's Day and he needed volunteers to staff the table. As class treasurer, I should have been scurrying around, trying to get people to sign up, but instead I sank into my chair. I didn't want to be reminded of last Valentine's Day, when Travis and I, both junior class officers, pinned construction-paper hearts on our clothing and paraded around the school selling red carnations.

Thinking about it now, it makes me shudder. But last year was the exception to my rule. I generally boycott anything to do with Valentine's Day. From late January until February 15, I'm prone to lousy moods and random fits of depression. I just hate how in the weeks leading up to V-Day, everyone gets all obsessed about my last name and people shout things at me in the hallway like, "Hey, Valentine!" and "Will you be *my* Valentine?" Call me the Ebenezer Scrooge of Valentine's Day. Bah-*freaking*-humbug.

Back to Travis. I was dreading Friday morning. That's when he and I were scheduled to meet with Mr. B about the Chemical-Free Grad Night party. We were the two cochairs, an honor bestowed upon us by the vice principal himself. So there would be no buffers, no bagels, no squirmy sixth graders to hog my attention. I knew I wouldn't be able to deal.

On my way out of school on Thursday, I dropped by the main office and asked Rosemary if I could speak to Mr. B.

"Anything for you, Mara!" she exclaimed, buzzing Mr. B on the intercom even though his office is nine feet from her desk.

Mr. B shook my hand and led me into his office. He was wearing his pea green polyester suit with the ink stain on the collar. On top of his bad taste in fashion, Mr. B makes that dire mistake of combing slicked strands over his bald spot, the ultimate optical disillusion.

As I sat down in the chair opposite his desk, Mr. B held the glass bowl of Hershey's Kisses in my direction. I shook my head and cut right to the chase, explaining how I had to resign as cochair of Chemical-Free Grad Night.

"But why?" he asked, frowning. "You seemed ecstatic when I invited you aboard last fall."

I wouldn't exactly say *ecstatic,* but I was still waiting to hear from Yale, so I may have played up my enthusiasm a little. Okay, I'll admit, I clapped my hands together, but I didn't jump up and down or anything.

"I'm just . . ." I paused. "I'm a little overwhelmed with my college classes."

Mr. B grinned. "If you're overwhelmed by SUNY Brockport, just wait until you get to Yale. *Then* you'll see what hard work is all about."

I looked down at my lap, totally sucking it up. *That's* how badly I didn't want to cochair with Travis.

"Well," Mr. B finally said, "while I'm sorry you can't help organize Chemical-Free Grad Night, I can hardly say no to you. Not with everything you've contributed to Brockport High School over the past four years."

"Thank you, Mr. B."

"Is there someone you can recommend as your replacement? Someone who has the same strong morals as you and Travis Hart?"

I nearly snorted at the mention of "strong morals" and

"Travis Hart" in the same breath, but Mr. B was waiting for a response. Maybe Bethany Madison? I hadn't returned her e-mail yet, so I don't know what's up with her, but I bet that's the kind of thing she'd like to do. *Hold on . . . no!* If I paired Travis with anyone of the opposite sex who wasn't hideously marred, he'd totally try something with them.

As I quickly mentioned a few guys in the senior class, Mr. B jotted their names down on a piece of paper.

To make matters even worse, things were getting weird at Common Grounds. Over the past week, whenever James stepped away from the counter, Claudia hunkered down with me and discussed Ways to Tell James She Loved Him.

"I'm just not smart the way you are," she whispered as we were discussing the possibility of writing him a letter or an e-mail. "I couldn't make it poetic and deep and meaningful."

"That's not true," I said. "But I can help you write it if you want."

"That's just like . . . isn't there an old Steve Martin movie where he does that?"

"All I know is the play, Cyrano de Bergerac."

"Cyrano de *what?*" Claudia sighed. "See, what I mean? I'm not a genius like you. You're going to *Yale* next year. That's the kind of thing that would impress James."

"It's not about me, Claud. We're talking about *you.*"

"I guess you're right," she said.

But the weird thing is that it *was* starting to feel like it was about me. While Claudia was finding every opportunity to chat with James, he was paying more and more attention to me. Last Saturday he told me he liked how I did my hair. I informed him that this is how I've always done it, blow-dried and tucked behind my ears. But he said, "No, no, it looks different."

On Thursday, when the baked goods were delivered, I discovered that James had added something to the inventory. Apple-nut cookies. *Vegan* apple-nut cookies.

"So there's finally food for Mara to eat," he said.

Several times throughout that shift, James and I made eye contact. We'd smile at each other and then I'd get that thump in my stomach so I'd look away quickly. But even so, I found myself highly aware of his physical presence when he was reaching over me for stirring sticks or lids or sugar packets.

Stop it! I'd tell myself. *Stop it and work harder at helping Claudia with her game plan.*

On Saturday, the solution finally presented itself. Claudia had turned twenty-one earlier in the month and, while we'd stuck a candle in a cranberry muffin and sung "Happy Birthday," she still hadn't ordered a drink from a bar. She'd complained about it so frequently that on a Saturday night in late January, James said, "Maybe we should grab a beer after work? You can order."

Claudia played it cool and was like, "Yeah, that'd be great."

But as soon as James went out to his car to get something, she squealed, "I'm going to do it! Tonight's the night! I'm going to do it!"

As she scavenged through her bag for lipstick, I asked if she knew how she was going to tell him.

"I'm just going to say it. Point-blank. What's the worst that can happen?"

"Good idea," I said.

Claudia was a wreck for the rest of the evening. She spilled coffee all over the counter. She dropped three slices of crumb cake. She gave a customer a ten-dollar bill instead of a one.

I tried to distract her by pointing out our favorite Internet mismatch. The beanpole mama's boy and the butternut-squash-shaped mama. It was their third date here, at least when we've been working. They were sitting with their faces close, licking blueberry cheesecake off each other's forks. Any other night, Claudia would have come up with all these funny comments about them. But she was busy obsessing about the fact that she wasn't dressed for a night out with James and maybe she should borrow my car and dash over to her dorm room to change into something sexier.

"It doesn't matter what you wear," I said. "James knows what you look like."

Claudia clutched my arm. "Oh my God. It's really going to happen! What do you think he'll say? Do you think he likes me back?"

"You'll find out very soon," I said.

But Claudia didn't find out. Toward the end of the shift, James walked over to her and said, "Do you mind if we do the beer another time? I'm exhausted. I think I'll just go home and crash."

Claudia shook her head and said, "No, that's fine."

But a few minutes later, when James was in the bathroom, Claudia sank onto a stool. "It's over," she moaned. "It's all over."

"What are you talking about? You can always do it another time."

"I've lost my nerve. I told myself that tonight was now or never."

I felt like such a hypocrite, but as I stood there patting her freshly brushed hair, I was relieved that the beer and confessional didn't happen tonight.

Don't ask me why.

I was refusing to even *go there* in my head.

chapter six

On the last Tuesday in January, the graffiti started showing up. As I was walking up the stairs between second and third period, I ran into Ash on the landing.

"Did you see it?" she asked.

"See what?"

"The second-floor girls' bathroom. Third stall."

"What?"

"I've questioned everyone and nobody knows who did it. It probably happened sometime between the end of the day yesterday and this morning. It's in permanent marker, so the janitors won't even be able to wash it off."

"What is it?"

"Go see for yourself!" Ash shouted as she disappeared down the stairs.

Third period was physics, a sink-or-swim subject, so I made myself pay attention as the teacher lectured about Newton's second law. But fourth period was my no-brainer psychology class. You could have a lobotomy and still get an A, so I asked for a bathroom pass and headed up to the second floor.

And there, in the third stall, written in black marker on the toothpaste-green wall, it said:

V VALENTINE IS A SKANKY HO!

Unbelievable. V has been here two weeks and she's already made the wall of shame. I considered scribbling it out with my pen. But it would be hard to conceal the marker with my measly ballpoint. And, besides, V has made this bed for herself—let her toss and turn in it.

The next day, after second period, I was in the basement bathroom checking my complexion. I'd broken out all over my forehead, so I'd carefully concealed everything with foundation that morning. I dusted some powder on my face and washed my hands. As I reached for a paper towel, I saw writing on the wall above the dispenser.

V VALENTINE IS A STONAH BABE!

It was in the same black marker, the same block letters. Who was the mysterious marker wielder? Besides me, who had it out for V already? Had she been hooking up with other girls' ex-boyfriends?

Knowing V, I wouldn't be surprised.

· · ·

At improv dance that afternoon, Dr. Hendrick told me that my stretches lacked effort. My jumping jacks could use more enthusiasm.

"And Ms. Valentine," he shouted over the drumbeat as we were supposed to be swinging our arms like elephants' trunks. "A smile couldn't hurt now and then!"

I was about to lose it. I really was. If we weren't a month into the semester, I'd totally drop this class and register for something else. I'd already decided to take it pass/fail, so the grade won't reflect on my final transcripts.

Twenty minutes into class, Dr. Hendrick instructed us to divide into groups of four and create a nature scene— one person as earth, one as wind, one as water, and one as fire. I was so paralyzed by the extreme cheesiness of the exercise that I didn't look around for three other people. And then, before I knew it, the class was all quadrupled up.

Dr. Hendrick sashayed behind me, rested his sweaty paws on my shoulders, and steered me toward the nearest group of four. "I hope you don't mind adopting Ms. Valentine," he said to them.

"But all the elements are taken," a college girl whined. I think her name is Rhonda. Her tags are always sticking out of her T-shirts. I've had a bad feeling about her from the first day.

"Why don't you just let Ms. Valentine be a rock," Dr. Hendrick said.

Anyone who has ever taken a dance class knows that being designated "the rock" is the equivalent of being "the tree" in a school play. It's totally like, *You are untalented deadweight so just shut up and petrify yourself.*

I curled into the fetal position on the stinky blue mat, wondering if I'm wound so tight I can't even dance.

On Thursday morning, as I was heading to homeroom, Ash caught up with me.

"I saw the new graffiti yesterday," I said before she could open her mouth.

"Which one?" she asked. "The one that says *stonah babe?* Because as of yesterday afternoon, there are four of those around school and two more *skanky ho*s."

"I saw the *stonah babe* in the basement. Who do you think is doing it?"

"Total mystery," Ash said, carefully enunciating her *t*'s.

"Has V pissed anyone off?"

"I haven't heard about any more locker-room encounters, but she's definitely generating gossip. She was all over Jordan Breslawski during an assembly on Monday afternoon."

"Lindsey's little brother? Isn't he a freshman?"

Ash nodded. "*Barely* fourteen. According to reliable sources who were sitting behind them, when the lights dimmed she put her hand, like, on his crotch."

I shuddered. The last time I'd talked to Jordan Breslawski was when Bethany and I slept over at Lindsey's house in ninth grade. Jordan had been wearing pajamas with old-fashioned planes on them and building an airport out of Legos.

Ash cracked her teeth on her Dentyne Ice. "But that's not what I was going to discuss with you this morning. I wanted to see if you knew about yesterday."

"Yesterday?"

"You didn't hear?"

I shook my head.

Ash smiled. "V ditched sixth period with Brandon Parker. They walked out the side door and went to his car. Three people saw them."

"Do you think they were . . ." I pinched my pointer finger and thumb in front of my lips and sucked in.

Ash shrugged. "Does Brandon do anything else? His mouth is, like, surgically attached to a joint."

We rounded the corner and paused in front of my homeroom.

"Have you seen any signs around the house?" Ash asked. "Pipes? Baggies of weed? Other drug paraphernalia? Have V's eyes been blurry or dilated?"

I knew I would make Ash's day, week, and month by reporting the oh-so-illegal scents wafting from upstairs, but I just shook my head and hurried into homeroom.

I decided to talk with my mom. After all, if V crashed and burned, I didn't want the lighter fluid on my hands. I wasn't going to give her specifics. I would croak before saying the words *skanky ho* to my mom because that would inevitably lead to highly uncomfortable questions such as:

> *Mom:* What's *skanky*, Mara?
>
> *Me:* Well, Mom, *skanky* is a term for a dirty slut who's riddled with sexually transmitted diseases. You know, a girl who'll drop her thong for every guy in school.
>
> *Mom* (most likely getting heart palpitations): *Riddled with STDs? Drop her thong?* And what about *ho?* Isn't that a gardening tool?
>
> *Me:* A gardening tool? Try *whore*, Mom. *Ho* is short for *whore*.

Thursday evening turned out to be the perfect night to talk. V had her first SAT prep class, so my dad drove her into Rochester. They left early because my dad wanted to stop by Digital Dynasty to get V a cell phone and add her to our Family Talk plan. When I heard that, I pulled V aside and whispered, "Who's got the umbilical cord now?"

She scowled at me. "Fuck off."

"Actually, that's your job," I said.

My mom made baked potatoes for dinner. She sprinkled cheddar and bacon bits on her potato. On mine, I loaded steamed broccoli and soy cheese, which is a sad substitute for cheddar, but I was trying not to think about it.

We were almost done with dinner when I asked, "How do you think V is doing so far?"

"How do *you* think V is doing?"

I picked at my potato skin with my fork. "I don't know," I said. "Some kids at school are saying things . . ."

"Saying things?" My mom frowned, the creases heading south on her cheeks. "About V?"

I nodded slowly.

"What could they say about V? She's only been here two weeks."

My thoughts exactly. "I'm not in the high school much . . . but I don't think she's making an effort to fit in. Why can't she try harder? Why does she have to have that attitude all the time?"

My mom sighed. "You've got to go easier on her, Mara."

"What do you mean 'go easier'? I've been fine. *She's* the one who's been hard on *me*."

I felt like crying. Did my mom have any idea how horrible V has been? What would she say if I told her V had fooled around with Travis Hart? It wouldn't just be palpitations. It would be a major heart attack.

My mom sipped her water. "All I'm saying is that V hasn't exactly had a smooth road. Did you know that Aimee hasn't called her yet?"

"What do you mean? Not since she's gotten to Costa Rica? Is she okay?"

My mom nodded. "Oh, she's fine. Dad sent her an e-mail last week to make sure she made it. She wrote him back from an Internet café and said there's no telephone where she's staying and she hasn't gotten around to buying a calling card."

"Typical Aimee."

"Right," my mom said. "Typical Aimee. But can you imagine if that were *your* mom? Can you imagine if Dad and I left you with relatives, moved out of the country, and didn't call for two weeks? Wouldn't you feel lousy?"

I stabbed a broccoli crown with my fork and dragged it across my plate to mop up stray shreds of soy cheese.

"Okay," I finally said. "Point taken."

Now that I'd semi-agreed to go easier on V, I absolutely *had* to steer clear of the house. So the next afternoon, rather than hanging around and risking an encounter, I put on my headphones and went walking. I hiked up the hill to Wegmans, back down the hill to the Erie Canal, over the bridge, and back again to Main Street.

Around five, it was starting to get dark. I turned off my music and wandered into Lift Bridge Book Shop. I frequently tempt myself by flipping through all the new novels I won't have time to read until, basically, I'm done with college.

I was only browsing for a few minutes when my cell phone rang.

"Mara?" my dad asked. "Where have you been? I've been trying you for over an hour. I've left three messages."

"I was just walking," I whispered. "I must not have heard the ringer."

"You should be more vigilant when you're out walking, Mara. You never know who—"

"I'm fine," I said, glancing around the store. There weren't many customers, but a woman was up at the cash register.

"I just wanted to tell you we're having a Family Meeting tonight. Right after dinner. You're not working, are you?"

"No," I said. "Why are we meeting?"

"We'll talk about it tonight. Where are you?"

"I'm in Lift Bridge."

"Be careful walking home. It's getting dark. Do you want me to come pick you up?"

"No, I'll be fine," I said.

I put my cell phone back in my coat pocket. That's when I noticed that the woman at the counter was looking over at me.

"Sorry," I said. "It was my dad."

She smiled. "We all have dads, right?"

As I was walking out of the bookstore, I couldn't stop thinking about how *most* of us have dads. But not V. Her biological father is some nameless guy who Aimee calls the Sperm Donor. Aimee once mentioned that V has his Irish nose and honey-colored hair. Another time, she told my mom that V inherited the Sperm Donor's ability to carry a tune. But that's all I've ever heard about him.

Sometimes, as much as I can't stand V, I kind of feel sorry for her.

My parents and V sat on the couch. I sat in the comfy chair on the other side of the living room. My mom started the Family Meeting by saying, in five different ways, how she and my dad are so happy that V is living with us. But then she pressed her fists into her lower back like she was massaging knots and said they needed to discuss a few "adjustment issues."

V hugged her knees to her chest. "Adjustment issues?"

It turns out my dad got a call from Mr. B today, informing him that V has been skipping some of her classes. V rationalized it by saying that a few teachers are being jerks to her because she's not caught up in the subjects. My parents offered to talk to them, but V was like, "No, no, I'll suck it up."

"Let us know if you're having any problems," my dad said. "We can always arrange for a tutor, if that would help."

V, still hugging her knees, started rocking from side to side.

"Sweetie," my mom said, "there's something else we'd like to talk about."

"We'd like to encourage you to get involved in a school activity," my dad said.

I nearly cracked up. V is always making fun of how

I'm a big joiner, but now *she's* getting a taste of life with my parents.

"A school activity?" V asked. "You mean like French Club?"

"Well, yes, that's an example," my mom said. "But something you're interested in. Somewhere you could meet people who share the same interests."

"But I don't really have any interests," V said.

"What about drama?" my mom asked. "You have a great voice and a knack for dancing . . ."

"Weren't you one of the leads in *Oklahoma!*?" my dad asked. "In your high school in Vermont?"

My parents were acting casual about it, but it was obvious they'd discussed this beforehand. I knew this scenario all too well. V was getting tag-teamed.

"Yeah," V said. "I was cast as Ado Annie, but it's not like I got to actually *be* in the play. Aimee made us move two weeks before it opened and the understudy got my part."

"What would you think about auditioning for the spring musical at Brockport High School?" my dad asked.

V paused. "Spring musical?"

My dad smiled at my mom. "When Ron Bonavoglia called me today, we got to talking. They're putting on a production of *Damn Yankees*. Auditions are in two weeks."

V shook her head. "I can't. What if Aimee comes back from Costa Rica and I have to move? I don't want to get my hopes up again. That sucked."

My parents exchanged a quick look and then my dad said, "Just think about it. You don't have to make any decisions tonight."

V started rocking again.

"Can I go now?" I asked.

My dad shook his head. "We wanted to talk with you, too."

"We were thinking about ways you can help V adjust," my mom said.

"Ways *I* can help?" I asked, glancing at V. She hugged her knees tighter and lowered her head.

"You've enjoyed working at Common Grounds so much," my mom said.

"Maybe you could get V a job there," my dad said.

NO! NO! NO! NO! NO!

"What do you think?" my mom asked.

I shook my head. "No way. Couldn't happen."

"At least talk to your boss about it," my dad said. "James seems like a decent person. Maybe he could—"

I rose to my feet. "No, okay? So just forget about it."

"Mara," my mom said, frowning. "I'm surprised at—"

I dashed toward the back door, grabbed my coat, and jogged down the driveway.

I walked all the way to Common Grounds. I didn't plan to. I just took a right on Centennial and a left on Main Street. As I neared the café, I spotted James getting out of his car. A second later, he glanced over and saw me.

"Hey, there!" he called out. "What are you doing downtown?"

"Just going for a walk," I said. "I needed to clear my head."

I noticed that James was smiling. I also noticed how broad his shoulders looked in his wool coat. Claudia has pointed out James's scrumptious shoulders on numerous occasions.

"Your cheeks are pink." James reached up and touched my face. "Why no scarf?"

"I . . . I sort of . . ." I paused. I couldn't stop thinking about how his hand felt on my cheek.

"Everything okay?"

I shook my head. "I left my house quickly."

"Angry?"

I nodded.

"Why?" James asked.

I glanced into the front window of Common Grounds to see who was working tonight. Okay, I'll admit it. I wanted to make sure Claudia wasn't there. It's not like I was doing anything *wrong,* but she may have taken it the wrong way, me standing on a dark sidewalk with James. I was relieved to see Josh and Randy, two guys who do a lot of shifts together, behind the counter.

I explained to James how V is living with us for a while. I was surprised to learn he actually knew that. He said that he overhead me telling Claudia. I told him how she's kind of a juvenile delinquent and how my parents had a Family Meeting tonight to discuss ways to help her adjust. When I told him they wanted me to get her a job at Common Grounds, James laughed.

"*My* Common Grounds?" he asked.

"Yep."

"What did you say?"

"Maybe I'm a horrible person, but I said no." I paused. "Do you think I'm a horrible person for not wanting her to work here? I bet that's what everyone thinks."

"Who's everyone?"

"I guess my parents."

"How do you feel about it?"

"I just feel like this is my place," I said. "I don't want V here, too."

"Well, sometimes you have to listen to yourself, even if it's not what your parents want."

James was standing pretty close to me. I got that thumping feeling again, so I stared down at the sidewalk.

"Want to come in and have some coffee or tea? Something to heat you up for the walk home?"

"No," I said. "I'd better get going."

James lifted both of his hands to my cheeks, holding them there for a few seconds. My heart started pounding so hard I could feel it in my entire chest.

"Stay warm, Mara," he said. And then he turned and headed inside.

chapter seven

The only good thing about early February was that Travis got mono and was out sick for two weeks. Okay, that's evil. I do not wish a fever and swollen glands on anyone. But it was a relief to not have him raising his hand in every class, hugging girls in every meeting. Plus, he'd missed a physics lab on the coefficient of friction and a pop quiz in psychology, so he was definitely losing that grade-point edge he'd gained when I bombed the government test.

I know that sounds thoroughly villainous. But I wanted valedictorian so badly, I could not only taste it; I could chew and swallow it. I couldn't stop imagining myself up at the podium in the gym, making the valedictory address, knowing I'd permanently bumped Travis to second place.

Bethany Madison was the one who told me about Travis having mono. On Wednesday of the first week that he was out, I was walking into the main office to drop off a National Honor Society roster and she was heading out.

"I'm sorry I didn't return your e-mail yet," I said as we paused in the doorway.

"I'm sure you've been busy, getting ready for Yale and everything."

"Have you heard from any colleges?"

Bethany shook her head. Her hair is Medusa-curly, so she usually pulls it back in a ponytail. "I've applied to Geneseo, Stony Brook, and Albany, but I won't hear until early April. I really want to go to Geneseo."

"I'm sure you'll get in."

"I don't know. I've got volleyball, but I'm not sure I have the grades."

"Grades aren't everything."

As I said that, I thought LIAR in my head. Look at me, jockeying for one-hundredth of a decimal point over Travis, feeling elated if I get it, feeling crushed if I don't.

Bethany must have read my mind because she whispered, "Did you hear about Travis?"

"You mean how he's sick?"

"Guess what he's got? *Mono.* The kissing disease! My mom ran into his dad in Wegmans. He's so weak he can't even lift his head."

"Poor Trav—"

"Don't bullshit me, Mara," Bethany said. "You're as thrilled as the next girl he treated like crap. He totally deserves this."

I smiled. Bethany started giggling, which made me start giggling.

As we were saying goodbye, I thought about how I've fallen out of touch with my high-school friends. It's not that I don't like them. It's that my mind is so focused on beginning my new life at Yale. And now that I've gotten accepted to the Johns Hopkins summer program and my parents mailed in the tuition, I'm leaving Brockport for good at the end of June. I feel like my mind has already gone and now my body just needs to follow.

My parents gave up on the idea of V working at Common Grounds, but they hadn't given up on V.

She had become their New Project, like reupholstering a couch or investing money in retirement funds. They quizzed her on SAT words. They looked over her homework. My mom was encouraging her to either grow out her bangs or get them trimmed.

V seemed to be gobbling up the attention. She didn't even protest when, last weekend, my parents called another Family Meeting, this one with the sole purpose of getting V to quit smoking.

As soon as the words were out of my dad's mouth, V jabbed her finger at me. "Did Mara tattle?"

My dad looked surprised. "No, sweetie. We knew you were smoking since last summer. Remember when you and Aimee visited and you had that lighter in your bag?"

"And I found an empty pack of Camels in your jeans when I was doing the laundry," my mom added.

It hit V and me at the same time. They were talking

about *cigarettes*, not the other kind of smoking. The illegal kind. I studied V's face carefully, wondering what she was thinking, but she wouldn't look in my direction.

V slumped back on the couch, sagging with relief that my parents weren't on to her. She was so relieved that when my parents lectured her about the horrors of nicotine — lung cancer, stained teeth, increased risk of strokes — V went up to her room, came down with two packs of cigarettes, handed them to my dad, and promised she'd never smoke again.

The biggest component of Project V was convincing her to try out for the school play. For two weekends in a row, my parents rented every musical they could get their hands on, from *Chicago* to *My Fair Lady* to *Moulin Rouge*. They even went so far as to go on to Amazon and buy the DVD of *Damn Yankees*. As soon as it arrived, my mom made a bag of microwave popcorn and the three of them watched it. I was in my room, proofreading some text for the yearbook, but I could hear them through my wall. They were rewinding and rewatching all the dance numbers. And every so often, they'd hit pause and remind V of her uncanny ability to carry a tune and her knack for dancing. Or they'd tell V that with all her energy, she belongs on a stage. Or they'd say that if she didn't have serious talent, she never would have gotten cast as a lead in *Oklahoma!*

I wasn't sure if anyone had spoken to Aimee yet, but one night, as I was brushing my teeth, I overheard my dad and V talking in my parents' bedroom. My dad basically gave V his word that if she got into the school play, she could stay with us through mid-April.

"But what if Aimee comes back from Costa Rica and I have to go with her wherever she moves?" V asked.

"Then we'll send you to Aimee *after* the school play."

"She'll probably come back, you know. This whole Campbell thing is so fucked up. He's a twenty-two-year-old surfer idiot. And, besides, Aimee can't commit to anything or anyone for more than a few months."

I strained to catch my dad's response, but all I could hear were his footsteps crossing the room and closing the door.

The next day, Aimee called. It was Wednesday, two days before Valentine's Day. I was home from school and had some time to kill before improv dance. I'd done all my homework, so I was working on the volunteer schedule for the senior-class candygram fundraiser.

Travis had sent me a brief e-mail that morning, saying he wasn't going to be back at school until the following Monday and asking if I could coordinate the V-day volunteers. I responded with an equally terse "Consider it done."

When the phone rang, I set my notebook on the coffee table and ran into the kitchen.

"Hello?"

"Mara?" Aimee shouted. The connection sounded crackly and distant. "I'm calling from a pay phone in downtown Jaco!"

"What's up?"

"Dad sent me two e-mails last night and one this morning telling me to call him. Is he around?"

"He's at his office."

"Oh, right, I'll try him over there." Aimee paused for a second. "Is my daughter there?"

"She's at school, Aim. It's early afternoon here."

"Why aren't you there? Exemption for geniuses?"

I ignored that comment.

"Listen," Aimee said after a moment. "I don't have a phone in my room, so can you tell V I'll call again soon?"

"Dad got her a cell phone," I said. "Want the number?"

Aimee laughed. "Did you just say that dad got her a *cell phone?*"

"We all have cell phones."

"Dad must love keeping constant tabs on everyone," Aimee said. "I bet it's making my daughter crazy. Are Mom and Dad driving her insane?"

"She actually seems okay," I said. I was thinking about how V has been laying lower at school recently. There's been no new graffiti, although the old stuff is still on the bathroom walls. But Ash hasn't stopped me all week, which is a good sign. And V has definitely been *looking* better now that she's officially growing out her bangs. She's been pinning them off to one side with a few barrettes. It looks cute, like from another era.

"Really?" Aimee asked. "She's doing okay?"

"Did Dad tell you she's taking an SAT prep course? She scored the highest of everyone on the English diagnostic yesterday."

"An SAT course? Are you serious?" Aimee laughed. "Before you know it, you'll *both* be going to Yale."

The way Aimee said it, it sounded like a bad thing. I decided to change the subject.

"How's Costa Rica?" I asked. "Are you learning to cook Central American cuisine?"

"I got a job at a restaurant but, you know . . . work's work. Doesn't matter what country you're in." Aimee paused. "I have some good news. Can you keep a secret?"

"I guess."

"I'm in love! His name is Campbell."

"Why's it a secret?"

"I don't want Mom and Dad getting all judgmental. Campbell's a full-time surfer. There's a whole group of them. They say they're going to Bali next and he wants me to come. Can you imagine? *Bali!* I don't know what—"

Suddenly there was so much static on the phone I could hardly hear her.

"I think our connection is breaking up!" Aimee shouted. "Tell V I'll call her soon."

I was about to ask again whether she wanted V's cell-phone number, but Aimee had already hung up.

I found myself thinking about James a lot those first two weeks in February. How his hands had felt when he'd touched my cheeks on the sidewalk, how his voice had sounded when he'd said, "Stay warm, Mara." He'd pop into my head at random times, like when I was sitting in government, listening to our teacher drone on about the presidential cabinet. Or when I was drinking a glass of water. Or when I was sleeping.

I'd been having dreams about James. For a few nights in a row, I had this one where we were behind the counter in Common Grounds, just the two of us, and then he'd walk into the supply room and I'd try to follow him, but the door was locked.

One evening—in real life, not in dreamland—I told Claudia we were low on paper towels and casually walked over to the supply room. On my way in, I quickly checked the door. I was surprised to learn that it didn't actually have a lock.

I found myself wishing Claudia weren't there. I know that's a terrible thought, so I didn't let myself linger on it.

Despite Claudia's proclamation that she was going to give up on James, she totally wasn't. She'd been wearing tight jeans and low-cut blouses to every shift in the hopes that he'd cash in that beer rain check.

That's what she was telling me on the night before

Valentine's Day. I was in a grouchy mood because two people in school had made dumb comments about how tomorrow is my big day. Around ten, James headed into the supply room to get the beans ready for roasting. With James out of earshot, Claudia cornered me and explained how she'd discussed the whole beer thing with her roommate, Pauline, who said that since he'd promised to take her out to a bar, he was definitely interested back.

"He didn't exactly promise," I said.

"What do you mean?" Claudia asked.

"He just said that maybe you guys should grab a beer."

"He did not!" Claudia flipped her hair over her shoulder. "He said, 'How about we grab a beer after work? You can order.' Pauline is a psych major and she told me that the fact that he said 'You can order' is an obvious clue that he was anticipating *being* there with me. It wasn't just hypothetical."

I restrained myself from telling Claudia that her roommate *must* be right because I'm only taking intro psychology and we haven't yet gotten to the unit where we psychoanalyze bar invitations.

"'You can order,'" Claudia said, punctuating each word. "Get it? 'You. Can. Order.'"

No, I didn't get it.

Nor did I get the fact that I'd been constantly dreaming about grilled-cheese sandwiches. I'd dreamed about them maybe once a month since I gave them up when I became a vegan. But these past few weeks, it was happening every night.

It was always the same. I was sitting at our dining-room table with a golden brown grilled-cheese sandwich in front of me. Cheddar cheese, white bread, lots of butter so it was extra crispy. It was cut diagonally down the center and when I lifted up one half, the melted cheese stretched like rubber bands to the other side.

Every morning when I woke up, my lips tasted salty.

chapter eight

On Valentine's Day, the Spirit Club plastered the school with red streamers and pink balloons and red and pink hearts. It looked like Clifford the Big Red Dog ate a flock of flamingos and then barfed his guts up. Four people made remarks about my last name, which actually wasn't as bad as previous years. It helped that I left school before noon. And it helped that I was in charge of the candygram volunteers. It gave me a distraction from all the smooching couples and girls carrying teddy bears and teachers handing out sugary hearts that said "Be mine" and "E-mail me."

V didn't seem as annoyed as I was by Valentine's Day. In fact, she got dressed up in her funky black pants and the I'M JUST A GIRL WHO CAIN'T SAY NO tank top. This time, she didn't hide it from my parents. They surprised me by laughing when they saw her in the kitchen. When

I asked what the big joke was about, my mom told me that that's a song Ado Annie sings in *Oklahoma!*

"That was my song," V said. And then she belted out, *"I'm just a girl who cain't say no. I'm in a turr-able fiiiiix."*

"V!" my dad exclaimed. "You have an amazing voice. You really have to—"

"I know, I know," V said. "I'm still thinking about it."

The following week, after a landslide of grandparental pressure, V tried out for *Damn Yankees*. My parents drove her to the audition on Monday evening and waited in the car outside. I was in the kitchen attempting to figure out what to eat for dinner when they got home.

"That was quick," I said as they came through the back door. "How did it go?"

"I fucked it up, so don't even ask," V said before stomping upstairs.

I glanced at my parents. My mom looked defeated. My dad said, "At least we tried."

But the next morning, right after Mr. B said the Pledge of Allegiance, Ms. Green got on the announcements.

"As many of you know," she said, "the drama club had auditions last night for the spring musical. The complete cast list is posted outside the main office, but I wanted to highlight our talented students who've been selected as leads."

I listened as T.J. Zuckerman, like every year, got the

male lead. And Brian Monroe, like every year, got the other male lead. I was waiting to hear that Andrea Kimball, like every year, got the female lead, when Ms. Green said, "I'm pleased to announce that the role of Lola has gone to a new student at BHS. Congratulations, V Valentine! We're happy to have you here."

I got goose bumps on my arms. I knew from catching enough glimpses of the *Damn Yankees* movie that Lola is the seductress who works for the devil. She's also the best part in the play.

Mindy Vance tapped my shoulder. "Isn't she, like, your niece or something?"

"Yeah," I said, nodding.

When the bell rang, I darted into the nearest bathroom. We're not supposed to use our cell phones in school, but I speed-dialed my dad.

"Did you hear?"

"Mom and I have both heard! V called us from her cell phone when she saw the cast list. She was crying."

V crying? Wow.

"It's a wonderful day for the Valentines," my dad said.

The day got even more wonderful when Mr. B summoned me into his office on my way out of school.

"I heard about your . . . errr . . . about Vivienne," he said.

I set my bag down next to my chair. "You mean V?"

"Ms. Green told me that she was highly impressed with her stage presence. I'm glad that Vivi . . . V was able to turn things around from her initial bumpy start. That's what we're about at Brockport High School. Second chances."

I glanced at the bowl of Jelly Bellies on his desk.

"I bet you're wondering why I called you in here," he said after a moment.

I nodded.

Mr. B raised his unibrow like a levitating caterpillar. "I wanted to talk to you about your grade-point average."

"My GPA? Everything's okay, right?"

Mr. B laughed. "Of course, Mara. We wouldn't expect anything less from you."

Phew.

"I imagine you know that third-quarter report cards are coming out this Friday."

I nodded.

"And I imagine you know that I already have those scores in my computer."

I hadn't known that, but I nodded anyway, just to hurry him to the finish line.

"And I imagine you know how close your GPA is to Travis Hart's."

Oh, yeah, maybe I knew something about that.

"You two have been neck and neck all year," he said. "In all my years as vice principal, I've never seen such a close race for the number-one class ranking."

Come on, come on!

"But I just wanted to say—and I'm going to speak

with Travis about this, too — that there are no winners or losers . . ."

Yeah, right.

"And whoever gets that second-place title has to remember that they are still number *two* in the entire class and they've still . . ."

I could barely stand it. I squeezed my hands into fists and bit down on my tongue.

" . . . made Brockport High School proud and they still are—"

"What's my GPA this quarter?"

Mr. B laughed. As he did, his long strands covering the bald spot slid precariously forward. "I can't reveal your exact grades, but as I said, I'm going to discuss all of this with Travis as well. I want you both to know how the next few months will play out. Toward the end of May, we'll get the remainder of your grades from your teachers, calculate everything, and determine valedictorian and salutatorian."

"So finals don't count?"

"Don't take this as carte blanche to blow off your final exams," Mr. B said, smiling. "But, no, we don't count seniors' finals in the GPA tally. We need to determine class ranking sooner, so we can print up graduation programs and so the valedictorian has time to prepare his"— Mr. B caught my eye—"or *her* speech."

I crossed my legs and started kicking my heel back and forth. "May I ask one thing?"

"Of course, Mara. Anything."

"Can I just ask how my new GPA stands in relation to Travis's?"

Mr. B took a deep breath before saying, "You inched ahead this quarter. Not by a lot, but if you continue to exhibit the same high-caliber work for the next three months, you will be our valedictorian."

I LOVE YOU, RON BONAVOGLIA!!!!!!!!!!!!!!!!!!!

I clapped my hands together. Mr. B held the bowl of Jelly Bellies in my direction. I helped myself to a green apple and two tangerines.

That night, my parents took us out to dinner in Rochester. We went to Aladdin's, which has falafel for me and red meat for V. V talked and laughed all throughout dinner, almost like a normal person. And she never once double-dipped her pita wedge into the hummus, as she's been known to do. At one point, while she was telling a story to my mom, I studied her face. With her hair pinned off to the side, I realized for the first time that our eyes are exactly the same shape.

On the ride home, my dad turned on some soft jazz. V leaned her head against the back seat. My mom put her hand on my dad's knee. I looked out my window at the snowflakes swirling around the side of the road. I had this bittersweet sad-happy feeling in my throat as I thought about how for once in a long time things actually felt okay.

chapter nine

Everything went to hell the last week in February.

My family always goes away that week. My dad has a five-day dental convention in Tampa that coincides with my school break, so my mom and I join him. We hang out by the pool and take a shuttle to the mall and invent names for all the shades of gray hair that we see on old people, such as *more-salt-than-pepper white* and *I-bet-you-can-guess-I'm-legally-blind blue.*

But I couldn't go this year. Even though high school was out for the week, I still had my college classes. Also, the yearbook pages were shipping to the printers in early March and I'd committed to proofreading all the text, an undertaking that was keeping me up past midnight every night. My parents had invited V to join them and it looked like she was going to go, especially since her SAT course was canceled over the school vacation. But then she got into the play and Ms. Green scheduled rehearsals for every day of break.

At first, my mom was going to stay home with us, but then my dad said that since he's probably retiring from dentistry in a few years, this may be one of their last chances to go. That's when they floated the idea of flying in my cousin Baxter Valentine from Portland. Baxter is in his thirties, still single, and a freelance cartoonist. All those hours alone with pen and ink have made him Extremely Weird. He visited us a few years ago and was perfectly normal in front of my parents, but as soon as they walked into the other room, he would make this screwy face at me and then bark like a dog or squawk like a chicken.

"No way!" I shouted when my parents called a Family Meeting and suggested inviting Baxter to Brockport. "Baxter is a freak!"

"No, he's not," my mom said. "He's a very successful —"

"Freak," V said. "When Aimee and I lived in Eugene, he drove down and stayed with us on the farm a few times. Maybe it was the Old MacDonald setting, but he was like quack-quack here, quack-quack there, here a quack —"

"Oh my God!" I shrieked. "Baxter made animal noises at you, too?"

V nodded. "Quacks, moos, barks . . ."

"Animal noises?" my dad asked.

My mom shook her head. "I can't believe Baxter makes —"

"Yes, he does!" V and I screamed at the same time. We could barely hold it together we were laughing so hard.

My parents finally abandoned the Baxter idea after V and I assured them we'd be fine and would eat well and lock the doors and go to bed at a decent hour. And so, on Monday morning of February break, they hugged us goodbye, extracted promises that we'd leave our cell phones on at all times, and headed to the garage.

"Parteeeee!" V shouted as their car backed down the driveway.

I eyed her suspiciously. "You're joking, right?"

"Duh, Mara," she said, and then headed up to her room.

I stood in the kitchen, trying to figure out whether that meant *duh, no* or *duh, yes.*

At first, it seemed like, duh, she *was* joking. V and I barely even saw each other on Monday or Tuesday. Some kids from the cast picked her up in the morning, and she didn't come home from play practice until evening, around the time I was leaving for Common Grounds.

I went over to the high school a few times to drop off pages of the yearbook and pick up the next section for proofreading. On Wednesday, Leesa Zuckerman held a meeting in the yearbook office. She's the executive editor, a junior, and T.J.'s little sister. Leesa gave updates on all the sections and then announced that the final vote on the title was "Breaking Out." It was an improvement over "Time of Our Lives," but I still didn't like it. It sounded like a prison escape or a raging case of acne. When I told this to Leesa after the meeting, she said, "You shouldn't read into everything so closely."

"I'm the proofreader," I said, "so you should hope I'm closely reading every word."

Leesa rolled her eyes. "Do you know if *anal-retentive* has a hyphen?"

"Very funny," I said, reaching over her for the sophomore-class section.

That afternoon at improv dance, Dr. Hendrick harassed me worse than ever. He kept shouting for me to "just let go and get into the movement." But every time he said it, I tensed up even more.

At one point, when we were supposed to be dangling like apples from a tree, Dr. Hendrick told the drummer to stop pounding.

"Ms. Valentine," he said as the room grew quiet. "You are a rotten apple."

Whenever he's made remarks like that in the past, I've always blown them off. But this time, I'd just had it. I lowered my arm/stem and looked him in the eye.

"Why don't you leave me alone?" I said. "I'm being the best apple I can."

The entire class/orchard stared at me.

"I don't like your attitude," Dr. Hendrick said.

"Well, I don't like your attitude, either," I said.

Then I grabbed my jacket and ran all the way out to my car.

• • •

On Friday afternoon, V got kicked out of play practice.

I was sitting at the dining-room table, still proofreading the sophomore-class section. I had my cell phone next to me because my dad had already called twice, first to ask if I'd eaten lunch and then to make sure I'd turned off the burners on the stove. My mom had called once to report that her favorite thing about Florida is that there are so many ancient people around she actually feels like a spring chicken, even though she's sixty-one.

I was just crossing out a caption that labeled Mr. B as *Vice Principle* and changing it to *Vice Principal* when V unlocked the side door.

"What are you doing home?" I asked.

"I got kicked out. I have to write a fucking letter of apology to go back tomorrow."

"You *what*? What did you do?"

"Why do you assume it's something *I* did?" V unlaced her boots and threw her bag onto the couch. As she headed up to her room, she said, "If you tell your parents, I'll murder you."

I sat there for a minute, clenching my pencil in my mouth, sinking my teeth into the soft wood. And then I dropped it on the table and walked upstairs.

V's door was a few inches open, so I pushed it forward. She was sitting on her bed, but when I came in, she jumped up and said, "What the fuck?"

I looked around the guest room. I hadn't been in here since V took it over. I was surprised to see that she hadn't fully unpacked. One of her duffel bags had shirts and jeans spilling out of it.

"I said, 'What the fuck?' Why didn't you knock?"

"Your door was open."

"It was slightly cracked."

I glanced at a small wooden object on her dresser. It looked like a miniature pipe.

V caught me looking and quickly slid a tissue box in front of it. "What do you want anyway?"

"I wanted to tell you that I didn't appreciate the death threat. I just asked why you got kicked out."

"It's none of your business, but someone pissed me off and I let him have it."

"Who?" I asked.

"I don't want to talk about it."

"Why can't you control yourself?"

V had unpinned her bangs, so they were hanging down to her nose. She angrily swept them to one side. "What the fuck do you mean?"

I felt this surge of adrenaline in my arms. "I mean, why do you have to say whatever goes through your head? Why can't you control your emotions?"

"Because I'm not repressed like *some* people."

I stepped closer to her. "What the fuck is *that* supposed to mean?"

"I can't believe you just said 'fuck'!" V shrieked. "I'm

going to call your parents and tell them we'll have to have a Family Meeting as soon as they get home."

"What do you mean 'repressed'?"

"Look in the mirror," V said. "You're the most repressed person I've ever met. You're so repressed, you can hardly even smile."

"I am not!"

"Why don't you ever let loose then?"

"You mean like a certain *loose* person?"

V stepped closer to me. We were only a few feet apart and the tension between us was palpable.

"Are you talking about the fact that I fooled around with Travis Hart?" V asked.

"You're the one who said it."

"Will you FUCKING let that go?" V screamed. "It was stupid and maybe I'm even sorry, but do you have to hold it over me forever? I mean, LET IT FUCKING GO!"

"I'll never let it go!" I screamed back. "It was a horrible thing to do and I'm never going to let you forget it."

"THEN GET THE FUCK OUT OF MY ROOM!"

"I'LL LEAVE WHEN I WANT—"

V shoved my shoulder. Then I shoved her, much harder than she'd pushed me because she stumbled backward. She had this shocked look on her face as she caught herself on her bedpost.

I bolted out of her room. When I got downstairs, I grabbed my car keys and peeled out of the driveway.

· · ·

I drove all the way to Lake Ontario. At first, I was too furious to even think. But after about ten miles, I started crying and biting my bottom lip.

When I reached the Lake Ontario State Parkway, I took a left, headed west, and drove through the entrance-way into Hamlin Beach State Park. I drove until I got to the first parking lot, which was empty, and pulled all the way up, so my car was facing the lake.

I cut the engine and sat there, staring out at the steely gray water. It was forebodingly rough and scratched with white caps. Lake Ontario is so immense you can't even see Canada on the other side. A few years ago, Bethany's dad took us sailing on the lake. We got so far out that we lost sight of the shoreline. I had this hyperventilating panic attack, but I was really discreet about it, so I don't think anyone even knew.

Is that what V meant when she said I was repressed? Or was she talking about physical stuff, like with Travis? I've never given her any details, but she pretty much got it right that first night she arrived, when she cornered me in the bathroom.

So maybe V is right. Maybe I am a repressed freak. Maybe I've got a genetic flaw, like Baxter, and I'll be single for my whole life and will terrify children by mooing and woofing at them.

My eyes were welling with tears. I looked up at the sea-gulls circling above the water. It must have been seriously windy out there because gusts kept flipping them over and propelling them sideways. I shivered. I was only wear-ing jeans and my Yale sweatshirt. I'd run out the door so quickly, I hadn't even grabbed a coat.

I can't believe I shoved V. I've never done anything like that in my entire life. I know she was being a bitch and she shoved me first, but when I picture her face as she stumbled across the room . . .

I started crying again. The air was so cold in my car that my cheeks were stinging. I wiped my face with the bottom of my sweatshirt and turned the ignition. As the heat came blasting out, I glanced at the clock.

Damn!

I'd completely forgotten about improv dance and now it was halfway over.

That night at Common Grounds, my wish came true.

"Claudia's sick," James said as I hung my coat in the cupboard behind the counter. "She called an hour ago. She's not coming in."

"Is she okay?"

"It sounds like the flu. . . . I'm sure she'll be better in a few days." James studied my face. "Are *you* okay?"

I thought I'd pulled myself together. When I got back from the lake, V was upstairs playing music. I'd taken a shower, blow-dried my hair, ate dinner, and headed over here. My eyes felt a little puffy and I'd launched a squeezing attack on a chin zit, but I'd carefully concealed it with foundation.

"I'm okay," I said. "Why?"

"You look a little upset."

I shook my head. "No . . . I'm fine."

"Why don't you sit down," he said, gesturing to one of the stools, "and let me make you a cup of Famous McCloskey Chamomint Tea."

"Famous McCloskey Chamomint Tea?"

James picked up two mugs and headed over to where we keep the jars of tea leaves. "A secret family recipe. It's a blend of chamomile, peppermint, a few other things. Cures anything from a broken heart to a bad-hair day."

I giggled. "A bad-hair day? Is that my problem?"

James smiled as he looked over his shoulder at me. "No, your hair looks beautiful."

For a second, there was this zingy-energy feeling between us. I quickly stared down at my hands. James turned back to the jars.

It was a blustery night, so we had very few customers. James made us two more cups of Famous McCloskey Chamomint Tea, which turned out to be the perfect blend of soothing and sweet. We sat on the stools, talking and laughing, stopping only to take turns heading to the bathroom. At one point, as I was washing my hands, I glanced into the mirror. My cheeks were flushed and my eyes were bright and my hair was messily falling in my face.

And guess what, V? I was smiling!

As I walked back to the counter, I pushed my hair behind my ears, but I couldn't wipe the smile off my face.

James and I talked about everything from Brockport to books to life in general. We ended up discussing these totally random things, like how annoying it is when you cut a tag out of your shirt because it's uncomfortable but then that little remaining strip itches you even more. Or why is it that soymilk always spills on the counter the first time you pour it, as if the people who manufacture it have never even tried it? Or why do people walk on the right in grocery stores, just like how we drive on the road? Did the walking come first and the cars follow? Or did cars dictate pedestrian patterns and, if so, how did people walk before cars came along?

Sometimes, like when we were discussing the walking question, we'd both laugh so hard that our legs would splay out and our knees would touch. It was only for a second, but it would send this tremor through my whole body.

After we'd talked for a while about how I'm going to Yale, I said to him, "May I ask you a question?"

"Sure."

"Why didn't you ever . . . Did you ever think about going to college?"

"My *parents* thought about me going to college."

"And you didn't want to?"

"I still want to," James said. "But I guess you could say I'm on the slow track. Toward the end of high school, when everyone was rushing off to college, I just wanted to experience real life."

"So how did Common Grounds happen?"

"After high school, I got my apartment in Presidents Village and a job at that Starbucks near the mall. And then, after a year of working there, I decided to try it myself. I applied for a small-business loan and learned the art of coffee roasting."

"What did your parents say?"

"They were upset for a while. You have to understand, I was an honors student, great SATs, swim team, the whole bit. They'd been thirsting for that Ivy League bumper sticker on their car."

Hmmmmm . . . sound familiar?

James quickly added, "This has nothing to do with anyone else's choices. I think it's amazing that you're going to Yale. This was . . . is . . . about me. I always seem to take my own time with things."

"What do your parents think now?"

"They won't stop bugging me for free bags of coffee!" James said, laughing. "I mean, I'm sure they'd love to see me go to college. But when I do it, it will be for me, on my own terms."

Neither of us said anything. I was thinking about what my parents would say if I told them I wasn't going to

Yale after all and had decided to get an apartment in Brockport. It's almost humorous when I picture their faces. *Almost.*

"You wouldn't believe this," James said, "but it's ten minutes past closing time."

I looked around. I hadn't even noticed that the few customers were gone, leaving mugs and plates scattered on some tables.

"Mara?"

I glanced over at James and was surprised to see that his normally calm face looked nervous.

"Yeah?"

"Do you ever think about . . ." James trailed off.

Yes, yes, I think about it, I answered him in my head. *I think about it a lot. But you can't say it. Because if you say it, then it's out there, and if it's out there, then . . .*

James shook his head and then reached over and tousled my hair in this brotherly way.

I couldn't help but feel a little disappointed.

That night in bed, I kept thinking about James.

STOP!

I flipped from side to side. I tried lying on my back. I tried lying on my stomach with my arms above me. I tried curling up with the pillow over my head. But no matter what I did, James wouldn't leave my mind.

STOP! STOP! STOP!

James is my boss, I'd tell myself. *He's twenty-two, the same*

age as Aimee's boyfriend, for God's sake. He's shorter than me.
He has no immediate college plans and he lives in an apartment
in Brockport and he graduated from high school when I was in
seventh grade. He has a ponytail. A short, pony-tailed twenty-
two-year-old high-school graduate.

Mostly, though, I was thinking about the fact that
Claudia loves James, which makes me a terrible, horrible,
no-good, very bad traitor. Worse than V because I didn't
even love Travis. But Claudia loves James. Even if it isn't
reciprocal, she loves him.

Then I'd tell myself, *No, no, I haven't done anything with*
James, especially not like what V did with Travis. So I'm still
innocent, right?

Right, I'd say. *You haven't done anything with James. You*
are innocent. Nothing has happened. NOTHING.

But as I lay awake in my bed, I was definitely thinking
about it.

chapter ten

My dad called four times on Saturday night. The first call came around seven, as he and my mom were driving across Tampa to dinner. After the usual did-you-eat-are-the-doors-locked questions, he asked if V was home yet.

"No," I said. "I think she's still at play practice."

Truthfully, I had no idea where V was. We hadn't seen each other since our fight yesterday. I was assuming she'd written her letter of apology and was back at rehearsal. But when I'd woken up, she was already gone and I hadn't heard from her for the rest of the day.

Three minutes later, my dad called again. "I reached her on her cell phone. She's at Pizza Hut with members of the cast."

"Oh."

"Is everything okay between you two?"

"Everything's fine. Don't worry."

"That's my job," my dad said.

Two hours later, he called again. He and my mom had just ordered dessert and he wanted to see if V was home yet.

"Not yet," I said.

"Have you spoken with her?"

"No."

"Are you sure everything's okay?"

"Yes," I lied.

Five minutes later, another phone call.

"V's at Friendly's," he said. "They went up there for ice-cream sundaes."

"That's nice."

If my dad heard the sarcasm in my voice, he didn't say anything. He told me that if V wasn't home by eleven, to call him back. As we were saying goodbye, he reminded me that they were catching an early-morning flight home, so if I needed to reach them, leave a message on his cell phone and he'd get back to me during their layover at JFK.

When I hung up, it hit me that a cell phone in the hands of the wrong person could be pretty annoying.

V didn't get home until after eleven, but I wasn't about to call my dad. I was sitting at my desk, organizing my folders so I'd be ready for school on Monday. Travis used to make fun of how I went through my binders every week and recopied notes that were messy and alphabetized articles and highlighted things that teachers said might show up on exams.

I heard a car pull into the driveway and voices in the

kitchen. A few minutes later, I heard another car and then another. The television blasted on. It sounded like the *Damn Yankees* DVD. As the smell of bacon wafted into my room, I finally headed out to investigate.

Five people were squished onto the couch and two more were pretzel-wrapped around each other on the comfy chair. None of them was V, but aside from a few scrawny freshmen, I knew most of their names. They were all drama-rama types. As they watched *Damn Yankees,* they were shouting out the lines along with the characters.

This junior named Nevin glanced up at me. "What are you doing here?"

"I live here," I said.

"You live here? In V's house?"

"Actually," I said, "V lives in my house."

Just then, the smoke detector went off and someone started shrieking. I ran into the kitchen and was momentarily taken aback by the chaos. Sneakers and boots and crumpled socks were all over the floor. Dishes and flour and eggshells littered one counter. On the other counter sat two more drama-ramas—Andrea Kimball shrieking and Brian Monroe sipping directly from the carton of orange juice. Ash Robinson—who'd been appropriately cast as the reporter in the play—was sitting on a stool. Leesa's older brother, T.J., was holding a spatula over a griddle of pancakes. The other frying pan, overflowing with bacon strips, was smoking like a volcano, but no one seemed to notice because all eyes were focused on V.

V, whose back was to me, was stretching a mop way up in the air and repeatedly whacking the smoke detector with the mop's stringy head. She whacked and whacked and whacked until finally it split open and the shrill alarm sound stopped. For a second, no one said anything. And then T.J. adjusted the heat on the bacon. Brian handed the juice to Andrea. V lowered the mop but continued looking up at the disabled smoke detector.

"Did you have to be so violent with it?" I asked.

V turned around and smirked at me. "Who are *you* to talk? You're Miss Domestic Violence!" She jousted the mop stick in my direction. "But you can't hurt me now because I am armed and dangerous."

"Will you quit it?" I hissed, glancing around. No one seemed to be paying attention except for Ash, whose eyes were ricocheting between V and me.

"I'm only teasing you," V said. "You just shoved me a little. It's not like I'm going to get a restraining order or—"

"Stop it!"

"You can't take a joke, can you?"

"No," I said. "I can't."

I headed into the laundry room and put on my coat and laced up my boots. I could see V mamboing behind T.J. and breathing heavily onto his neck. Andrea and Brian were getting into a debate about whether it's called a "pancake turner" or a "spatula." Ash was watching everything intently.

I grabbed my car keys and slipped outside. I'd been planning to drive around and listen to music, so I was annoyed to see three cars blocking mine in.

"Mara?" Ash peeked her head out the back door. "You okay?"

"Yeah."

"Were you going anywhere in particular?"

"Nope."

"V and T.J. sure seem to be hitting it off. I ran into Leesa in the mall last night and she said that—"

I cut Ash off. "I don't want to hear about V, okay?"

Ash stepped onto the driveway. "Why are you being so hard on her? Don't you appreciate how she stuck up for you?"

"Stuck up for me?"

The yard lights were on, so I could see Ash smile. "I'm sure you heard how Ms. Green kicked her out of practice yesterday."

"She told someone off, right?"

Ash hugged her arms across her chest. "That's putting it nicely. I've never heard so many four-letter words in my life. That choreographer looked like he didn't know whether to run for cover or strangle her."

"Choreographer?"

"Dr. Hendrick."

Oh. My. God.

I vaguely remember V mentioning that Ms. Green had

hired someone from the college to choreograph this year's musical, but I never for a second imagined it would be my sweat-soaked improv dance teacher.

Ash went on to tell me how at play practice yesterday, Dr. Hendrick was choreographing a complicated routine for V's first song. It's a funny number, so the whole cast was watching. When V got everything perfect on the first try, he made some comment about how V couldn't possibly be related to a "simply horrendous dancer by the name of Mara Valentine."

I sucked in my breath. "What did V say?"

"Well." Ash paused for emphasis. "V went totally *Godfather* on him. She told him—and enter about twenty swear words here—what she would do to him if he *ever* talked about one of her family members again."

"No way! That did NOT happen!"

Ash nodded. "Ms. Green said she felt bad kicking V out because Dr. Hendrick was completely inappropriate, but she had to set an example, you know, for the rest of the cast."

My head was spinning with confusion. I couldn't believe Dr. Hendrick had dissed me in front of the *Damn Yankees* cast. And V had defended me? I'd have guessed that she would have seized the opportunity to publicly trash me, to say that I wasn't only a bad dancer, but also a repressed baby who hasn't cut the umbilical cord.

Ash was staring expectantly at me.

"I'm going for a walk," I said.

Before Ash could get in another word, I headed down the driveway.

I knew exactly where I was going, but I wouldn't let myself think about it.

Instead, I burrowed my hands into my coat pockets and started walking. The sky was pinkish and overcast. The houses were dark and the sidewalks were empty and, aside from the occasional passing car, Brockport was asleep.

I took a right on College Street and a left on Main Street. I walked past the brick building where I went to nursery school and past Arjuna Florist, where I got Travis's boutonniere for the Winter Ball last year. I walked past Common Grounds, which was closed for the night, and past the post office where I sent off my Yale application. I paused in front of the massive iron lift bridge that spans the Erie Canal and connects Brockport's north and south sides.

I slowly crossed the bridge, careful not to look down at the wide gaps through which you can see inky dark water. The sidewalk was choppy as I walked down the hill on the other side, past Pizza Hut, where I'd had my final bite of cheese before I became a vegan. Finally, I rounded West Avenue and headed into Presidents Village.

I'd been to James's apartment once before. Last spring, Claudia and I went over to pick up our paychecks when the computer at Common Grounds was broken.

Claudia. I couldn't think about Claudia right now.

I walked along the narrow path until I found the right apartment. It must have been after midnight, so I knocked lightly on the door, almost hoping James was already asleep.

"Yeah?" James's voice said after a moment.

Oh God. Oh God. Oh God.

"Is somebody there?" he asked.

"Me," I said. My throat was so tight it came out like a squeak.

Silence.

"Mara?"

Yes, Mara. I have come to your home in the middle of the night. I am insane.

I heard footsteps crossing the floor and then the lock clicked and a groggy-looking James was standing in the doorway. His hair was loose around his shoulders and he was wearing a long-sleeved gray T-shirt and faded jeans with a nickel-sized hole in the thigh.

"I'm sorry," I said. "Were you sleeping?"

What was I saying? Of course he was sleeping!

James shook his head and said, "No, no, that's fine." But then he let out this lion-size yawn.

I had to laugh.

He smiled. "Okay, maybe I was. But I fell asleep reading on the couch, so it's not like I went to *bed* or anything."

"I was just going for a walk and I thought—"

"You don't have to make excuses," James said, grinning. "I know why you're here."

"What?"

"You want another cup of Famous McCloskey Chamomint Tea. McCloskeys have come to expect this over the years. You give someone one cup and then, every day, they're knocking at your door. But that's why we only share it with people we like. So come on in . . . I'll make you a cup."

"Are you sure?"

James opened the door wider. I stepped into his apartment. He reached behind me and took off my coat. As he did, his hands lingered on my shoulders for an extra second.

James hung my coat over the back of a chair. "I'll be in the kitchen. Make yourself comfortable."

I took off my boots, lining them up neatly by the door. Then I padded into his living room, which was filled with more books than Seymour Library. I sat on the couch and folded my legs under me. There was an open copy of *The Poisonwood Bible* on the couch. Very interesting. When we were talking last night, I told him that that was my favorite Barbara Kingsolver novel. He said that although he owned a copy, he'd never read it. Even more interesting is that I drove over to Lift Bridge this morning and bought *High Fidelity* because James had told me last night that it was his favorite Nick Hornby novel.

James carried two mugs into the living room. I couldn't help but notice how his shirt stretched across his broad shoulders. I glanced at the hole in his jeans. I had this sudden urge to touch it. I sat on my hands.

James placed one mug on the table next to me, pushed *The Poisonwood Bible* off to the side, and joined me on the couch. He leaned over and set his cup on the floor at his feet.

"Do you like it?" I asked, gesturing to the book.

"It's hard to get into, but I have a feeling it's going to be worth it."

"It's definitely worth it," I said.

The hole in James's jeans was on the far side of me, out of my direct line of vision, so I freed one hand and reached for my tea.

"It's really hot," James said. "You might want to give it a little more time."

I put down the mug and set my hand on my lap. We were both staring straight forward, like passengers on an airplane. It felt awkward, which is weird because James and I are usually so comfortable around each other. But then again, we've never been alone in an apartment in the middle of the night with one of us wearing jeans with a hole in the thigh.

"You know," James finally said, "I put on one of those tag-cut-out shirts today and it itched me so much I had to take it off. I thought of you."

"That's so funny," I said, "because I opened a new box of soymilk this morning and it splashed out of my cereal bowl and I thought of *you*!"

James laughed. "It's nice that we think of each other in such special moments."

"I thought of you other times, too." As soon as I said that, my heart skipped a beat, realizing how it sounded.

James leaned over and picked up his mug, taking a careful sip. When he set it back down, I could swear he shifted his body a tiny bit closer to me.

"Is it snowing yet?" he asked.

I shook my head.

"We're supposed to get twelve to fourteen inches tonight."

"Really?" I asked. "That many?"

James nodded.

Silence.

My feet were falling asleep, so I stretched out my legs. As I did, I shifted my body a tiny bit closer to him.

"I like your apartment," I said.

"Thanks. You've been here before, right?"

I nodded. "Last spring, when I came with . . ." I paused. "When I came to get my paycheck."

"Oh, that's right. The computer at Common Grounds was broken."

"Right."

More silence.

We were talking in these stilted sentences, but it felt like there was meaning behind every inflection. I was hyperaware of James's legs, his arms, and especially how his hand was currently sliding onto the empty spot on the couch between us.

I lowered my hand so it was about three inches from his.

And then James did it.

He reached over and put his hand on top of mine, interlacing his fingers with my fingers. I turned my hand over, so our palms were touching. Neither of us made a sound. I don't even think I was breathing.

James leaned toward me. I leaned toward him, closing my eyes, still holding his hand. When our lips met, we held them still for a second. His hair brushed against my cheek. He tasted sweet, like chamomile and mint. As he parted his lips, I parted mine. We pressed the tips of our tongues together and then closed our mouths again.

James stroked the back of my neck, sliding his hands along the slopes of my shoulders. I was about to melt into his arms when this thought jolted me like an alarm clock on a predawn morning.

CLAUDIA! OMIGOD! CLAUDIA! OMIGOD! CLAUDIA!

I pulled back from James and dropped his hand. *I am horrible. I am worse than horrible. I am —*

"What's wrong?" James asked. His eyes were crinkled with concern. I'd never seen his eyes so close up, never realized they had ambery flecks in them.

I shook my head. "We shouldn't be doing this."

"We don't have to. If you're not comfortable, then —"

"I've got to go." I stood up quickly and raced into the foyer.

"Can you tell me what's wrong?" James asked, following me.

I double-knotted one boot and then the other.

What's wrong is that I'm a backstabbing traitor. What's wrong is that I never should have come here and now I need to get out before it's too late. What's wrong is that every additional second I remain here I become an even more horrible person.

James handed me my coat. "Can I at least give you a ride home?"

"I'm fine walking," I said.

He filled his cheeks with air and slowly deflated them. "Are you sure?"

I nodded and took off out his door.

I barely remember the walk home. It had started snowing. Heavy, wet flakes. My throat felt scratchy and dry. I was so drained I couldn't even think, which was probably a good thing . . . considering.

The one thing I do remember is that as I retraced my steps through all the familiar streets of my life, I now felt completely lost.

chapter eleven

When I woke up in the morning, my throat hurt so badly
I couldn't swallow. It took me a few seconds to remember
what had happened last night, and when I did I was over-
come with shame.

There was an intense light penetrating the curtains
next to my bed. I rolled over and peeked out the window.
Snow was everywhere, so white it was almost blue. Mounds
and ripples heaped over parked cars, weighing down the
shrubs, turning front lawns into glaring mirrors.

I closed the curtain and yanked my blanket over my
eyes.

I am a horrible person, I thought. *Horrible, traitorous,
backstabbing. I have been the one encouraging Claudia to go after
James all this time. I am a horrible, horrible, horrible person.*

I must have fallen back asleep. When I woke again,
my throat hurt even worse. The phone was ringing, but

someone picked it up. Probably my mom or dad. No, if they'd gotten home from Florida, they would have come in and said hello. I wondered what time it was. I was too tired to look at my clock.

I drifted off and was awoken again by the phone. My sinuses were clogged. My joints and muscles hurt. All I wanted to do was sleep. Sleep and forget about how awful I felt. Sleep and forget about last night.

Someone knocked at my door.

"Come in," I croaked.

"Are you okay?" V asked. "You sound like you're sick."

I squinted at her. Her hair was pulled into a high ponytail. She was wearing plaid pajama bottoms and one of my dad's old sweatshirts.

"Aren't you supposed to be at play practice?"

As V shook her head, her ponytail swung from side to side. "Canceled because of the blizzard."

"What about my parents? Have you heard from them?"

"They've been calling all morning. The Rochester air-port is closed, so they're stuck in New York City. They can't get a flight out until tomorrow, and they can't even find an available hotel room."

"What are they doing?"

"Your mom said they were staying with Mike and Phyllis."

"Oh . . . the Shreves." We see them every few years. My mom and Mike grew up in the same town outside of

Boston. Their families were friends and my mom used to baby-sit for Mike when she was a teenager.

"Your mom said that Aimee and I went to the zoo with their daughter, Virginia, when I was little, but I don't remember."

I didn't say anything. My throat hurt so badly, I felt like I'd swallowed shattered glass.

"Can I get you anything?" V asked after a moment. "Juice or water?"

I shook my head.

"I guess I'll let you get back to sleep."

V pulled the door closed but didn't shut it the whole way.

I must have fallen asleep again because the next time V came into my room, I was having a stress dream. I don't even remember what it was about, but I could tell I'd been grinding my teeth.

"I'm sorry to wake you up," she said. "I told your parents you were sick, and your dad said you should drink echinacea tea, so I made you a cup of it." V set a mug on the coaster on my bedside table. "I didn't put honey in because I wasn't sure if vegans eat honey."

"Thanks," I said. I was surprised she knew about that, how some vegans think eating honey is exploiting bee's labor. I don't happen to be one of those vegans, but I appreciated the gesture.

V chewed her thumbnail. "I thought you'd like to know

117

that I fixed the smoke detector. I even tested it with a match and it still works."

I wasn't sure what to say. I pulled my blanket up to my shoulders.

V glanced around my room. "Mara?"

"Yeah?"

"I'm sorry for what I said last night . . . the whole domestic-violence thing. Sometimes I have a big mouth. It was a dumb thing to say."

"You were just joking. Sometimes I can get too sensitive." I paused before saying, "I'm sorry I shoved you."

"I'm sorry I shoved you, too."

I felt choked up. V had this pinched look on her face, like she was going to cry. She started out of my room. As she reached the doorway, I said, "V?"

She turned around. "Yeah?"

"Thanks again for the tea."

"No problem."

I dozed for the rest of the day. A few times I got up to pee or eat applesauce, but all I wanted to do was crawl back into bed.

In the early evening, I was propped up with some pillows reading *High Fidelity* when the phone rang. A moment later, V peeked into my room.

"It's James from Common Grounds," she said. "Do you want to pick up?"

My stomach lurched. I'd been trying not to think about what had happened with James, but when V said his name, I wanted to hide under my covers and never come out.

"No," I said, quietly. "Tell him I can't talk. Tell him I'm sleeping."

I was sick for most of the week. We had a snow day on Monday, so I didn't miss school. When my parents got home from the airport that afternoon, they made me drink two cups of echinacea tea and take about a gazillion milligrams of vitamin C. Even so, I felt like hell on Tuesday, so my dad drove V over to the high school. My mom called the main office and asked Rosemary to tell my teachers to send my assignments home with V.

I slept on and off all day, waking only to blow my nose. When V got home, she dropped off a pile of homework on my desk, but I didn't even look at it. My head was drowning in so much mucus, I could barely think.

By Wednesday, I still felt crappy but I got up to e-mail the teacher who coordinates tutoring sixth graders and told him I wouldn't be able to make it. Then I sent an e-mail to my statistics professor at the college and explained why I missed class yesterday and said I would probably miss again tomorrow. I knew I should e-mail Dr. Hendrick. I had now missed three dance classes in a row, not counting the one I had bolted out of, but I just didn't want to deal.

I was about to get up from my desk when an IM from TravisRox188 appeared on my screen.

Haven't seen u in a few days, he wrote. *R u sick?*

Yep.

Excellent. Now I'll be able to catch my GPA back up w/ yours. Ha-ha-ha-ha.

U r a merciless jerk, I wrote back to him.

Thanx 4 the compliment. Get better . . . but not 2 soon.;)

I didn't even write back. Instead, I blew my nose and sipped some water and flipped through the assignments that V had brought home for me. If Travis thinks he'll catch up with me that easily, he's got another thing coming. I stayed at my desk for two hours and even read a chapter ahead in my government textbook, until finally I collapsed in an exhausted heap on my bed.

On Thursday morning, I finished *High Fidelity* and wanted to call James to tell him how much I loved it. But I couldn't. I still hadn't talked to him since Saturday night. I'd been scheduled to work a few shifts throughout the week, but on Monday I'd left a message on the voice mail at Common Grounds saying I'd be out sick indefinitely. I left it early in the morning, when I knew no one would be there. Not James. Definitely not Claudia.

James had left two messages on my cell phone. I had seen both of them come in on caller ID, so I didn't pick up. Of course, I listened to the messages as soon as he left them. They were brief, just asking if I was feeling better and saying to please call him at home if I wanted to talk.

No, I did not want to talk. Could not talk. Didn't know

what to say. I wasn't even sure I could ever *see* him again. The temptation might be too strong. And the guilt would definitely be too overwhelming.

I wouldn't allow myself to think any good thoughts about James. Whenever he came into my mind, which was a lot, I'd tell myself that James is Hands-off. Private Property. No Trespassing. I'd remind myself that James is twenty-two. That he was a café owner when I was in ninth grade. I'd think about how James didn't even go to college. How James lived in Brockport. How all I wanted to do right now was fast-forward out of this town, not make new connections here.

But when I fell asleep, the good thoughts wended their way in. I'd dream about James's laugh and the feel of his lips. I'd dream about his shoulders and the shape of his fingernails and the way his butt fit into his worn jeans. One time, I even dreamed about touching my finger inside that hole in his jeans.

I woke up from that dream with my heart racing so fast I couldn't fall back asleep for over an hour.

In my dreams, I'd also expanded my cheese repertoire. On a nightly basis, I was dreaming about the mozzarella sticks they serve at Friendly's. I was dreaming about greasily delicious Pizza Hut pizzas with green peppers and olives on top. I was dreaming about quesadillas smothered in guacamole.

In the morning, I would tell myself I couldn't go on

this way, that something had to give. I would tell myself that I'd made choices in my life, good choices, and now I had to live with them. I told myself these things so many times throughout the day, I almost believed it.

But then, every night, the dreams came back.

chapter twelve

Sometime before dawn on Friday, I reached over to my bedside table for a tissue and got that weightless yank that comes with the last one. I'd been so congested all week, I'd gone through an entire box. I blew my nose, but as I dropped the tissue in the trash basket next to my bed, I sneezed again. So I pushed back my covers and headed to the laundry room to get a new box.

As I was walking back to bed, I paused in front of the dining-room window. The grayish light was just burning through the night sky. The snowdrifts that had been plowed to either side of our driveway were still shadowy and dark. The birds hadn't yet arrived at our feeder for their morning seed-fest. But looking out the window, there was this sense that everything was about to happen.

A random thought drifted into my mind. So maybe I *am* repressed. Maybe I hold the reins too tightly and don't know how to let loose. But I can't imagine it's a terminal condition. With the right person, maybe I could learn to give up some control.

There's no way it could have happened with Travis, who prodded and coaxed me until being with him was more of a battle of the wills than anything intimate or romantic. And it's not going to happen in Dr. Hendrick's dance class, where he badgers me to let loose, forces me to be someone I'm not. Because the bottom line is that I don't want to be a gazelle or an apple dangling off a tree or whatever other idiotic things he thinks will bring out my inner free spirit.

I sneezed three times in a row and headed back to my room, where I slept until my alarm went off forty-five minutes later.

Despite my water-faucet nose, I felt better enough to go back to school that day. I made it through all my classes with a mini-pack of Kleenex on my desk. After fourth period, I headed to my locker to retrieve my coat and bag. But rather than going straight to my car, I paid a quick visit to my guidance counselor.

Her name is Roberta Kerr, but among seniors she's the Gateway to College. She's the one who helps compile your transcripts and test scores and recommendation letters for college applications. She's the one who will put in a call to the Office of Admissions at your top choice if she thinks you're an extra-special candidate. It's crucially important to be on Ms. Kerr's VIP list. Thankfully, I am.

We small-talked for a minute and then Ms. Kerr said, "So what's up?"

"I'm going to drop the improv dance class I'm taking through 3-1-3. I just wanted to make sure it won't affect my final GPA or show up on my college transcripts."

"Mara, I'm surprised to hear you say this. What's wrong with the class?"

I shook my head. "I just don't like it."

Ms. Kerr rotated her chair around to the wall of filing cabinets. She pulled out my folder and thumbed through the contents until she came to SUNY Brockport letterhead.

"It's too late in the semester to switch to another class," she said after scanning the paper. "You have enough credits to graduate, so it'll be no problem there. And if you officially drop the class, it won't show up on any transcripts. But the problem is that since you'll only be taking one college class this semester and you took two last semester, you'll just have three college classes when you go to Yale. As you know, the goal of 3-1-3 is to have taken four."

"I'll be taking two more courses at Johns Hopkins this summer," I said. "Remember that precollege program I applied for?"

"Oh, yes." Ms. Kerr quickly flipped through more pages of my file. "Yes, of course."

"So that means I'll enter Yale with *five* college courses."

Ms. Kerr pressed her lips together. "Are you sure about this? When we admit people to the 3-1-3 program, they are representatives of Brockport High School. Anything they do reflects on us, so therefore we do not encourage or condone dropping a class." She paused before adding, "Even if you don't like it."

How could she say this to me? I have been a freaking *ambassador* for this high school for nearly four years! At Model UN, yearbook conventions, leadership conferences. I raised the mean SAT score for my class by several points. I got into Yale, which not only reflects positively on the high school but on her job as well. How is it that I can perform with flying colors a thousand times, but then I stumble once and I'm vacuumed off the red carpet?

"Yes," I said. "I'm sure about this."

"I assume you've discussed this with your parents?"

No, I had not discussed this with my parents. If I had, they would have talked me out of it for sure.

"Yes . . . they said it's okay."

"Well, then." Ms. Kerr cast a disappointed look at me. "If you're certain about this, I'll send an e-mail over to the college registrar and let them know you're dropping."

After I left her office, I stopped in the bathroom across the hall. My nose had gotten so clogged I needed to give it an all-out honking blow. As I was throwing a wad of tissues into the trash, I saw those square black letters:

V VALENTINE IS AN STD! THAT MEANS SLUTTY TRAMPY DEGENERATE!!!

I'd actually seen this one before. It had appeared that first week the graffiti showed up and, according to Ash Robinson, it was hands down the cruelest. I remember being amused that whoever wrote it was smart enough to spell *degenerate* correctly. But now it hit me how awful it is that someone trashed V all over the bathroom walls. Sure, she got off to a less-than-savory start, but why can't people cut her a little slack?

I headed up to my locker, where I rummaged through my pen basket until I found the permanent marker that I used for making the sign above the candygram table. I walked back to the bathroom and quickly scribbled over the graffiti until I couldn't read a single word. Then I dashed down to the basement bathroom and up to the second-floor bathroom and into every other bathroom that Ash had told me about, scribbling and scribbling until there was nothing left but long black rectangles and smudges of ink all over my fingers.

My mom came into my room on Sunday afternoon. "How about a drive to Letchworth?"

"Letchworth?" I asked.

That's this state park about forty miles south of

Brockport. They call it the Grand Canyon of the East because it's a dramatically deep gorge with gushing waterfalls. We usually go hiking there in the fall when the foliage is blazing.

My mom nodded. "I thought it would be nice to get out of the house for a while. It's sunny, the roads are clear, and I've finished my work."

I hadn't been doing much, just going through my CDs and weeding out the ones I never listen to anymore. My mom had been working on a fundraising letter in her room, and my dad and V had just left for Rochester, where V had a marathon five-hour SAT review course.

"Okay," I said. "Why not?"

Twenty minutes later, we were heading south on Route 19. My sniffle was considerably better, but I'd stuffed several tissues in my coat pocket. My mom put some music on. I stared out my window as the flat landscape gave way to more and more hills. It was early March, a few weeks before the start of spring, but the trees were still skeletally bare and the cornfields were blanketed with snow.

We'd been driving for about thirty minutes when my mom turned the volume down. "You've been quiet," she said. "Anything on your mind?"

"Not really."

"Can you believe you have less than six months until Yale?"

I shook my head.

"We should plan a trip to the mall soon, get some sheets and towels for your dorm room. You'll need them this summer, too, in Baltimore."

I shrugged. I didn't feel like talking about college or summer academic plans, even though it's the number-one way my parents and I relate.

"Have you figured out what courses you're registering for at Johns Hopkins?" my mom asked. "I was flipping through the catalog the other night and everything looks so fascinating."

I shook my head again. When I first got accepted, I'd read the course catalog from cover to cover and dog-eared pages about international affairs and neuroscience and bioethics, but I hadn't picked it up for several weeks.

"It's so amazing to think that between SUNY Brockport and Johns Hopkins, you'll have six college classes under your belt by the time you get to Yale. And then factor in your AP classes. I hope they accept all the credits and advance you to second-year status."

I got this anxious feeling in my stomach. I still hadn't told my parents about dropping improv dance. I'd been planning to detonate the bomb all weekend, but every time I came close, I thoroughly chickened out.

"Are you sure there's nothing on your mind?" my mom asked.

I shrugged again and looked out my window.

We didn't say much for the rest of the drive. I continued staring at the snowy fields and the blink-and-they're-gone towns along Route 19. We finally reached Letchworth and drove along the main road until we got to the parking lot where we usually start our hikes.

We pulled our hats down over our ears and our scarves up over our noses and started toward the trailhead. But thirty steps later, a stinging wind blasted across the parking lot. We grabbed each other's hands and mad-dashed back to the car, careful not to slip on any ice.

My mom turned up the heat and we pressed our fingers in front of the vents. As we were warming up, we got kind of giddy. It all began when we joked about what my dad would do if the state troopers called him to say we'd been discovered, frozen solid, in a Letchworth parking lot. Of all my dad's paranoid fears about harm that could be brought upon his family, Parking Lot Danger ranks near the top. He's constantly reminding us to watch out for drivers who zigzag across empty spaces and runaway shopping carts and, of course, predators who hide behind parked cars.

We were still laughing when my mom gasped, "Oh my God!"

"What?"

She pointed her finger across the nearly empty parking lot, where a silver SUV was two rows up and three rows over. I stared at it for a second before noticing that, prominently displayed on the bumper, was a sticker that proclaimed MY CHILD BEAT UP YOUR HONOR STUDENT. It was in the exact same colors and font as the bumper sticker on my mom's car, which of course says MY CHILD IS AN HONOR STUDENT.

I cracked up. "Do you think I'm in imminent danger?"

"If we see them, I'll take off. Let's just hope they don't notice the Yale sticker on the way out!"

Neither of us said anything for a moment. I blew my nose and then glanced at my mom. "Remember before, when you were talking about college classes?"

She nodded.

"There's something I have to tell you."

"What?"

"You know that improv dance class?"

"You mentioned something about the teacher. You don't like him, right?"

"*Didn't* like him. I dropped it on Friday, which means... It means I'll only graduate with three college credits. But I'll make it up at Johns Hopkins this summer and can still hopefully get second-year status in the fall."

"Why didn't you talk with us about it?" she asked.

"I thought you and Dad would tell me to stick with it, and I've just been feeling like . . ." I paused. All the thoughts I've been having are so new right now. I didn't know how to say them out loud. Or even whether I wanted to.

"Why do you think we'd tell you that?"

I ran my fingers along my seat belt. "Because of Aimee. How she dropped out of college. I didn't want you to think you'd have to go through that whole thing again."

My mom shook her head. "I may have suggested you talk to the teacher, but I wouldn't push you to do anything you hated."

"But I always feel like you're so worried about how Aimee has turned out, like I'm the daughter who has to do it all."

My mom didn't say anything for a minute. It was weird. I'd been contemplating these things for practically my entire life, but I'd never actually voiced them out loud. I wasn't sure how I'd feel if she confirmed it and said something like, *Yes, Mara, you are our only hope, so don't screw it up.*

Finally, my mom said, "We don't talk about this much . . . about you . . . about *how* you . . . came to be."

Was she talking about what I think she was talking about?

I didn't know whether to disappear into my seat or shake the words out of her as hard and fast as I could. I have never talked to my mom about how *anyone* came to be. She was totally understating it when she said we don't talk about it much. We don't talk about it AT ALL.

My mom's cheeks flushed. "But I think you should know that Dad and I . . . We didn't . . . You weren't . . ." She quickly touched her hand to her face. "I was forty-three when I had you and I'd already started menopause, so I didn't think I could get . . ." My mom paused before saying, "What I'm trying to say is that we didn't have you to compensate for Aimee."

"Hold on," I said. "Are you saying I was a *mistake?*"

"Let's call it a surprise."

I was too shocked to even be embarrassed by the fact that my mom just disclosed to me that I was an unplanned pregnancy. I'd always assumed I was brought into this world to give my parents award ceremonies and Yale bumper stickers and everything that Aimee didn't provide them.

My mom continued. "I'm just telling you this so you don't feel pressure to 'do it all,' as you said. Of course, Dad and I are proud of your accomplishments and the high standards you have set for yourself. But we love Aimee just as much as we love you. We *do* wish she'd gone to college and we wish she'd given V a more consistent upbringing, but she's still our daughter and we love her no matter what."

I stretched my seat belt out as far as it would go and let it zip back in again. "What if I changed my plans and didn't go to college? What if I decided to live in Brockport and work at Common Grounds full-time?"

My mom laughed, like I was making a joke. I remained quiet.

"I'd be surprised," she finally said. "No, I'd be shocked. But it wouldn't change how I feel about you. I wouldn't love you any less."

That was all I needed to hear. I let out a long, slow breath.

"You're just being hypothetical, right?" my mom asked. "You're not *really* planning to defer Yale?"

"Right," I said laughing. "Purely hypothetical."

We spent the next hour driving around Letchworth, past the Glen Iris Inn and the Mary Jemison statue and the high railroad trestle. We didn't talk about anything much, just pointing things out along the way.

As it was getting dark, my mom's cell phone rang. It was my dad, telling her that V had another hour of SAT prep and then they were going to eat in Rochester. After they said goodbye, my mom asked if I wanted to grab dinner on the way home.

I was definitely getting hungry, but the only restaurants between here and Brockport are roadside diners where it's nearly impossible to find anything vegan. Every salad has bacon bits, every mashed potato has butter, every soup is made with chicken stock. It's frustrating for me, but I also hate driving waiters crazy, asking about the ingredients of various items on the menu and then just ordering a bowl of kidney beans and raw broccoli.

My mom must have read my mind. "No vegan options?"

I nodded. "It's so annoying."

"Do you ever think about not eating vegan?"

I shook my head. "I don't think I'll ever eat meat again. Eggs still gross me out, too."

"So you think about dairy?"

"Cheese," I said. "I think about cheese sometimes."

Talk about understatements! I CRAVE cheese. I LUST after cheese. I DREAM about cheese.

"You know, Mara," my mom said, "sometimes we make decisions about our life and they feel like the right decision at the time. No, they *are* the right decision at the time. But that doesn't mean they'll be the right decision forever. And you know what I've realized as I've gotten older? There isn't a definite right and wrong anyway. Sometimes we do what *seems* wrong, but we have good reasons for doing it, so it's not wrong after all."

I think she was referring to the whole vegan thing, but as she spoke, something else was flooding my brain. No, not something. Some*one*. Someone with a chestnut ponytail and an easy smile and a hole in the thigh of his faded jeans. Someone who would not leave my thoughts no matter how many times I tried to evict him.

When V hooked up with Travis in January, I remember being convinced that there was a right and a wrong and you couldn't cross that line no matter what. Just like how I've been telling myself that I can't think about James because he belongs to Claudia and because he's older and shorter and lives in Brockport and and and . . .

It suddenly dawned on me. I don't regret kissing James last weekend. It was oh-so-very wrong. But at the same time, nothing has ever felt more right.

"I hope that makes sense," my mom said. "Maybe it's just something everyone has to figure out on their own."

"No," I said, "it definitely makes sense."

Once those words were out of my mouth, I realized that I was willing to cross that line. For whatever reasons, good or bad, I was willing to cross it with James.

I had to talk to him. IMMEDIATELY.

I glanced at the speedometer. My mom had the car on cruise control, two miles below the speed limit. I was tempted to tell her to step on the gas.

chapter thirteen

My dad and V were still out when we got home, which was a good thing because it meant I didn't have to go through any paternal Q&A. I grabbed my cell phone and car keys and told my mom that I just remembered I had to pick up some yearbook stuff from a friend's house. Luckily, she didn't know that the yearbook pages went to the printers last week. All she asked was whether I wanted to eat before I left, but I told her no, I wasn't hungry, and then I hurried out the door.

I took the back streets downtown. When I was a block from Common Grounds, I pulled off to the side, shifted into park, and dialed the café. I didn't think Claudia was scheduled to work tonight, but I figured I'd just hang up if she answered.

"Common Grounds," James said.

I could hear coffee grinding and milk steaming and voices booming. It sounded like Josh and Randy. They frequently work on Sundays. They're two of the loudest guys I've ever met.

"James?" I asked.

"Mara? Hey there! Are you feeling better?"

"Yeah . . . much better."

I could hear Josh bellow, "ONE CHAI, ONE NON-FAT LATTE," and then Randy responded, "COMING RIGHT UP!"

"What's up?" James asked. "You sound like you're on your cell phone."

"I'm in my car." I paused. "I was just wondering . . . Can we talk?"

"Of course. When's good for you?"

I glanced at the clock. It was after nine on a school night, but I just couldn't wait. I'd waited long enough and I didn't want to go to sleep tonight without talking to James.

"How about now?" I asked.

"On the phone?"

"I was more thinking in person . . . if you can get away."

"Hold on a second."

I could hear James saying something in the background. I heard Randy say, "YOU TAKE YOUR TIME!" And then Josh added, "WE'VE GOT EVERYTHING UNDER CONTROL HERE, BOSS-MAN!"

"Where do you want to meet?" James asked.

"I can pick you up in front of Common Grounds."

"When should I head outside?"

"Right now. I'm a block away."

James laughed. "I like your style."

I put the car back into gear and took a left on Main Street. James was already in front of Common Grounds. He was just wearing a wool sweater and jeans, but not the ones with the hole in the thigh, which was probably a good thing because I really *did* want to talk and that hole seemed to obliterate my ability to think.

I slowed down. James ran over to the passenger side and hopped in. We both said these bashful *hello*s to each other and then he buckled his seat belt and I started driving again. I asked James where he wanted to go, and he said anywhere was fine. I suggested Clarkson Playground because it was in the direction my car was heading and I doubted anyone else would be there on a chilly March night. James said that sounded fine. He spoke quickly, like he was nervous, and I wanted to tell him not to be nervous, but I was nervous, too, so I just concentrated on the road.

After a few miles, I turned into the playground parking lot. It's one of those gigantic wooden wonderlands with tire swings and metal slides and plank bridges. A lot of people from my high school come out here to party on warm nights.

I cut the engine and turned off my headlights. James and I stared out at the silhouettes of playground equipment.

"It looks kind of creepy at night," he said.

"I know."

"When I was in high school, people used to get drunk here."

I laughed. "They still do!"

"It's funny how those kind of things don't change in five years," James said.

Neither of us spoke. It was like having those two words—*five years*—in the air between us brought us up-to-date on the fact that we'd kissed, that we had this big age difference, that we'd come out here to talk.

"Is that what you've been thinking about since last Saturday?" James finally asked. "That I'm older than you?"

"Among other things."

"Me, too." James unbuckled his seat belt and turned toward me. "You want to go first?"

"With all the things I've been thinking about?"

He nodded.

"Okay," I said. "I've been thinking about the fact that I'm leaving Brockport for good in June."

"Yep," James said, "less than four months away."

"And it's definitely weird on paper."

"You mean that you're still in high school and I'm twenty-two and own a café and I'm shorter than you and I didn't go to college and you're going to Yale?"

I had to laugh. James was ticking things right off my mental list.

"And it would be weird working together," I said.

"You mean Claudia?"

My mouth felt dry. "You know about Claudia?"

"I've never talked about it with her, but I've sensed for a while that she might be . . ." James squinted out at the playground. "Remember when we were supposed to have a beer a month or so ago?"

I nodded.

"That's why I canceled. I didn't want her to get the wrong idea. Especially since I was . . ." James fiddled with the latch on the glove compartment. "I was wondering what was going on with you."

My heart went THUMP! and I got this major adrenaline rush, like if I went out to the playground I'd make it all the way across the monkey bars even though I haven't been able to do that since puberty hit and I grew eleven inches.

"Phew," James exhaled loudly.

I stared down at my shaking hands.

"What are you thinking?" he asked.

"I'm just thinking that this is so weird."

"I know."

"But I'm also thinking how . . ." I paused. "I was wondering what was going on, too."

"You were?"

I nodded. "But it just feels like . . . How could it ever work?"

"And what would people think?"

"And what would we do about Claudia?" I was quiet for a moment before adding, "And I'm scared."

"Of what?"

I shook my head. I was thinking about so many things . . . my bad experience with Travis, my parents, Claudia, doing the wrong thing, doing the right thing. And especially this sense I had that being with James could quite possibly change my entire life and I wasn't sure if I was ready for that.

Finally, I turned toward James. "But I still want to try."

"You do?"

I nodded.

We both reached out and took each other's hand. We didn't say anything for a second as we smiled and tilted our heads closer and closer . . .

And then my cell phone rang.

I grabbed it out of my coat pocket and glanced at the caller ID. It was my dad. I hit the "cancel" button and set it on my lap.

"Sorry," I said.

"No, that's fine. Do you have to go home?"

I shook my head.

We leaned toward each other, our lips meeting over the emergency brake. It started out a soft kiss, but after a little while, we opened our lips wider and our tongues began venturing into each other's mouths.

My phone rang again. I pulled back for a second and

glanced down in my lap. Another call from my dad. This time I turned the phone off, dropped it in my coat pocket, and went back to kissing James.

We didn't leave Clarkson Playground until ten-thirty. I would have stayed even later, but James said he had to close Common Grounds or at least let Josh and Randy go home. When I dropped him off in front of the café, we kissed on the lips and I told him I was sorry it had taken me so long to call. He said that a week isn't that long.

The whole drive home, I kept thinking how good it felt to kiss James and how I was already counting the minutes until the next time I could see him. But as I turned onto our street, I was jolted out of my dreamy haze.

Practically every light in my house was on.

When I'm working late at Common Grounds, my dad usually just leaves the yard lights on. But now our entire house was illuminated by thousands of watts of parental worry. I pulled into the driveway and nimbly closed my car door in case, for some bizarre reason, my parents had simply forgotten to pull the plug when they went to sleep. But before I could even put my key in the lock, my dad opened the back door.

"Where. Were. You." His jaw was clenched and his normally windblown hair was hurricane wild, as if he'd spent the past few hours repeatedly running his hands through it.

"I was at Bethany Madison's," I said. I used to spend a

143

lot of late evenings at her house in early high school. "I'm sorry I got home so—"

"Mom said you were picking up something for the yearbook. Since when has Bethany been on the yearbook staff?"

SHIT! So much had happened in the past few hours, I'd completely forgotten about the yearbook excuse. And I was totally being haunted by the fact that I used to tell my parents *waaaaay* too much about my life. I mean, my dad knows who's on the yearbook staff?!

"Since this year," I lied.

My dad nodded skeptically. "What did you pick up?"

I didn't feel like digging myself deeper into the deception, so I just said, "Nothing after all."

My dad paced across the kitchen. I could see V sitting on the couch in the living room.

"Where's Mom?" I asked.

"She went to bed. She wasn't as worried as I was."

"Why were you so worried? I've stayed out later than this before."

The muscles in my dad's jaw were twitching. "I was worried because you didn't answer your phone. Didn't you get my calls?"

"My phone was in the car." That was the truth, actually. I just didn't mention that *I* was in the car, too.

"Why would you leave your phone in the car?"

I raised and lowered my shoulders.

"The whole reason you have a cell phone is so we can

144

reach you if we're worried. So we can make sure you're okay."

"But I was fine."

"I didn't know that. I didn't know where you were or what you were doing, and it was after eleven on a school night."

I glanced at the clock. It was only two minutes after eleven, but I wasn't about to tell that to my dad. Nor was I about to tell him the other thing I was thinking, which is that when I'm away at college, he can't expect to tuck me in every night. That he needs to start letting me go, so the empty-nest thing doesn't come as a huge shock.

"Mara," my dad said, "you have to keep your cell phone on you when you are away from the house. We need to be able to reach you."

I did *not* want to be having this conversation right now. All I wanted to do was go into my room and be alone and think about what had just happened with James.

"Okay," I said, sighing. "From now on I will surgically attach my phone to my bellybutton."

"Your bellybutton?"

"You know, like an umbilical cord. From you to me and me to you."

"I'm not being cute," my dad said. "What's gotten into you?"

I shook my head. "Nothing. I'm just tired. Can I go to sleep now?"

My dad nodded. I dashed into my room. I was only

there for about thirty seconds when V approached my doorway.

"Hey," she said.

"Hey."

"I've never seen G-pa like that. He was pacing all over the house before you got here."

"What did my mom say?"

"She told him to relax. She said she trusted you. He said he did, too, but it was the rest of the world he didn't trust. They didn't exactly get into an argument, but she definitely looked like she was losing her patience with him."

"Did she happen to mention anything about college classes?"

V shook her head. "No . . . why?"

"Never mind."

I was definitely relieved that, on top of everything, my mom hadn't told him I'd dropped improv dance. It's weird. I've always thought of my parents as this single-brained, two-bodied unit, where one is an extension of the other. But recently they've been seeming more and more different. I feel like my mom is giving me the space I need, while my dad is holding on so tight he's smothering me.

"I think I know what's gotten into you," V said.

"What are you talking about?"

"When G-pa asked what's gotten into you . . . I think I know. I think you're falling in love."

"No, I'm not! I was at Bethany Madison's house."

146

V smiled. "Very interesting . . . so now you're a lesbian."

I had to laugh. "Do you think that's why my dad was freaking out?"

"Definitely. He's already picturing himself marching in gay-pride parades."

"Very funny."

After V said good night, I glanced in my mirror. My lips were a little puffy from all the kissing. I gathered my hair back and fastened it with a rubber band. For the first time in years, it's almost long enough to put into a ponytail without any pieces falling out.

I suddenly realized I was famished. I hadn't eaten since before Letchworth. There'd been so many other things on my mind, I'd been ignoring my empty stomach.

I tiptoed through the now-dark house and into the kitchen. I didn't even turn on the light as I leaned against the counter, tearing off pieces of pita and dipping them into the plastic container of hummus. Okay, I'll admit it, I was double-dipping. But no one else really eats the hummus, so I figured it was not *that* sinful.

Yeah, sure, said a voice in my head. *Next thing you know you'll be drinking right out of the orange-juice carton.*

chapter fourteen

V was right. I was falling in love. James and I were falling in love. It had only been three days since Clarkson Playground, but I could tell in the way we looked at each other.

Plus, we were doing all those things you hear about when people fall in love, like blowing air kisses and pretending to catch them on our cheeks. And quoting sappy songs because for once the lyrics actually made sense. And asking about each other's scars and siblings and middle names. James's middle name was Herbert, which made me laugh so hard I actually started gagging. I ceased my choking long enough to tell him mine, Elizabeth, and when he responded with, "That's so beautiful," I apologized for laughing at Herbert, but he said, "No, no, I'm still not sure whether my parents realized they'd had a baby and not a cartoon dinosaur."

We also talked about serious things, like past relationships. It all started when we were on the phone late Monday night, after everyone else in my house had gone to sleep. I was lying in bed, running my fingers up and down my arm.

James was telling me how that evening at Common Grounds, a light bulb blew in the bathroom and no one could reach it, even when they were standing on their tiptoes on a stool. Finally, they had to borrow a ladder from Lift Bridge across the street.

"If you were there you definitely could have gotten it," James said.

"I am the Queen of Changing Bulbs. You have to be when you're tall because everyone always asks you."

"What a royal honor."

I stopped touching my arm. "Have you ever dated someone who's taller than you?"

James laughed. "Oh, no! The past-relationships question!"

"You don't have to . . ."

"No, it's good to talk about it . . . have it out there and over with. You want me to go first?"

"Sure."

James told me how he'd had two big relationships in his life. One in high school, with a girl named Jessica. And one when he was twenty with a college student named Christie. They were together for a year, but now she lived in Pennsylvania and their only communication was jokes she forwarded to him and thirty other people over e-mail.

"And to answer your question," James said, "they were both shorter than me."

"Does it feel weird that I'm—"

"*Mara Elizabeth.* Nothing about you feels weird. I like you just the way you are."

"Isn't that a Billy Joel song?"

"Very good," James said, laughing. "But I'm serious. I like that you're different from anyone else I've been with."

"I feel the same way," I said, suppressing a giggle, "James Herbert."

"Stop it!"

"It's just so tempting."

"Now your turn. What about your ex-boyfriends?"

"There's not much to tell."

"I've heard you talk about one . . . that guy you're competing with for valedictorian."

"Right . . . Travis."

"Why'd you break up?"

I was about to give him my stock answer—*We just didn't click*—but instead I decided to tell the truth. I told him how Travis pushed me to do things I didn't want to do. I told him how Travis once made fun of the size of my chest. I told him how he eventually dumped me because I wouldn't go all the way with him.

"Guys can be such jerks sometimes," James said.

"Not all of them. Not you."

"Do you know that I would never push you to do anything you didn't want to do?"

"I know."

"Good."

I have to admit, I was relieved to hear that because, as we were discussing exes, I couldn't stop thinking about the fact that James *is* twenty-two. And I have a feeling that by the time people are in their twenties, they're not exactly walking in slow numerical order around the bases.

But the ironic thing is that when we were alone together, all I wanted to be doing was kissing and James was the one who recommended we take a breather. On Monday, Tuesday, and Wednesday, I'd gone over to his apartment after school. We mostly kissed on his couch, but we'd also kissed in the foyer and the kitchen and the middle of the living room. I'd peeked into his bedroom once, but we'd never gone in there. Sometimes I wanted to. Like, when we were on the couch and James was kissing my neck. Or when I nuzzled my head into his shoulder and he hugged his arms around me. Those were the times I wanted to press my whole body against him. But instead I'd kiss his mouth with all the intensity I was feeling inside and he'd kiss me back, and we'd kiss and kiss until James would finally suggest we put on our coats and walk over to the duck pond near his apartment.

I left from these afternoons with James still tasting

him and smelling him and feeling his lips. The whole first part of that week, I walked around in this fog of *JamesJamesJamesJamesJames*. I barely even concentrated on my homework, just did what needed to get done and not even the bonus questions. When we had a senior-class council meeting on Wednesday to decide the theme song for the prom and people voted for Boyz II Men's "End of the Road"—which, in my opinion, is a dumb choice because it's the ultimate breakup song—I didn't care enough to speak up.

Around the house, I tripped on chair legs and lost my train of thought in the middle of sentences. It was probably because I was so tired. The past three nights, James and I had stayed up late, talking and laughing on the phone, until we both said good night and then I slipped into a dreamless coma.

If my parents knew something was up, they didn't let on. My dad and I had struck a careful peace on Monday evening. I'd apologized for not answering my cell phone the previous night and he'd said he was sorry for being so hard on me. Then I'd told him about dropping improv dance. He'd said the same thing as my mom, that at least I was taking two college courses this summer.

Later that evening, my mom came into my room and asked if I felt okay about what she'd told me at Letchworth. I said yes, that it's actually a relief to know. She nodded and then quickly changed the subject to whether we should have brown rice or basmati rice with dinner.

I never once mentioned James to my parents. I liked it that he was All Mine. My boyfriend. My choice. My life. Not the subject of a Family Meeting or any other form of Valentine scrutiny.

All day Thursday, I had a queasy stomach and a constant pulsing in my temples. That night was the first time I was going to work at Common Grounds in nearly two weeks. Not since I'd first kissed James at his apartment and then I'd gotten that cold and then I'd avoided him and now we were together. But we'd never been together around Claudia, and I was so nervous about it, it was making me sick.

When I met James at his apartment that afternoon, he was actually the one to bring it up. He asked how I thought we should handle our relationship at work, even offered to talk to Claudia. But I shook my head and said, "No, no, no!" Claudia would DIE if James talked about that with her. Not to mention that she'd probably take me with her on her way out. And, besides, we'd only been together four days and everything still felt new and special. I didn't want to screw it up with some huge drama. When I explained it that way, James said he understood, so we agreed to be low-key at Common Grounds, at least for a while.

That evening, James spent a lot of time back near the roaster. I think he was trying to keep his distance. I was actually grateful for that because whenever he was nearby I wanted to touch him and whisper *Herbert* in his ear.

Even so, I was feeling definite tension with Claudia. She kept snapping coffee orders at me and telling me to hurry up with the cash register. At one point, toward the end of the night, I walked back to the roaster and asked James whether I should brew more coffee or just use up what we've got.

When I returned to the counter, Claudia said, "What were you talking about?"

"Nothing."

"It couldn't have been nothing because your lips were moving."

"I just asked if we should brew more coffee."

She smacked her hand on her hip, which was jutting obstinately to one side. "Is that all?"

I nodded. Claudia turned brusquely away from me.

On Saturday night, things got even worse. It was a busy shift, full of Internet daters. Practically every couple looked like they were on a blind date, from the way they bickered over who would treat to how they zealously exclaimed, "You like chocolate, too?!!" when one of them ordered fudge cake.

Claudia and I were so crazed, it almost felt like old times, especially since James was out most of the evening running errands. So that's why, just after I served this lesbian couple—identical short haircuts, identical silver earrings, identical jeans, identical burgundy shirts—I tapped Claudia's arm and whispered, "Thirty-six-year-old woman seeks her identical twin for closet rummaging and much, much more."

Claudia jerked her arm away from me and didn't say anything. But then, a few minutes later, she said, "How about this one? Twenty-two-year-old café owner seeks high-school student for jailbait and much, much more."

I felt like I'd been smacked in the face.

"Well," Claudia said. "True or false?"

"Is what true?" I asked nervously.

"Are you and James interested in each other?"

I stared at Claudia. My pulse was racing and my hands were clammy. She had this furious look on her face, like she wanted to pummel me. I felt so caught off-guard, I didn't know what to say.

"Don't worry." I took a shallow breath. "Nothing's going on."

"Promise?" Claudia asked.

"Yeah . . . I promise."

chapter fifteen

All through March, lies were pouring out of my mouth as steadily as the skies were dumping sleet onto western New York.

When Claudia asked why I was yawning so much, I told her that teachers were slamming seniors with homework. When V questioned me about an oblong splotch on my neck—one word: *hickey*—I told her I'd burned myself while I was straightening my hair. When Ash Robinson noticed I'd written *James Herbert* in tiny letters on the corner of my government notebook, I said he's a Supreme Court judge. And whenever my parents called my cell phone on school-day afternoons, I'd tell them I was studying in the college library even though I was usually on James's couch.

After that first call, James and I had a long talk about my parents. I told him how they've basically made every decision for me in my life. I said that this time around I want to listen to my heart and do what feels right for me. Not to mention that if they knew James and I were together, they'd immediately jump to the wrong conclusion about what a twenty-two-year-old could possibly want from their innocent little girl. James said that I knew my dynamic with my parents better than anyone, so it was my decision how much I wanted to tell them. He jokingly asked whether my dad owned a shotgun and, if so, had he ever pointed it at his daughers' suitors? I told him that my dad's only weapon was a dental drill. James cupped his hand over his mouth and moaned, "Even worse."

One part of the lying that was getting weird was Bethany Madison. As far as my parents were concerned, Bethany and I had been hanging out a lot recently. She and the college library were my standby excuses whenever I wanted a few hours with James. Unbeknownst to Bethany, we'd studied together, gone to two movies, and shopped at Marketplace Mall.

But I was starting to get paranoid about the fact that, other than waves and smiles in the hallway, Bethany and I had not gone to the library or the mall or the Strand Theater. I couldn't help but wonder if my parents were noticing that Bethany wasn't calling or coming over to our house and I returned from shopping empty-handed and with that hickey on my neck.

One Thursday in late March, V bailed me out on the Bethany front. I was working at Common Grounds. Claudia was, too, but had to leave early to meet up with a study group for her literature class. As soon as she was gone, James asked if I wanted to stay late with him. After the café closes every Thursday, he roasts the coffee beans for the week. He does it at night because he uses this old-fashioned roaster that puffs smoke and rumbles like a bad muffler. Last week, I kept him company over the phone while he was roasting and made him describe every step to me as he went along.

"Now I'm pouring in the green coffee," he said. "That's what you call beans before they are roasted."

"What kind are you making?"

"Costa Rican Tarrazu. It's best at a medium roast, so I'll take it out after the first crack."

"First *what?*"

"That's the sound a coffee bean makes when it's roasting. For a medium roast, you take it out after one crack. For a dark roast, after two."

"How long will this batch take?"

"About thirty-five to forty minutes."

"That long?"

"A large commercial roaster will churn them out in ten minutes, but it's really compromising on quality. I like to roast them slowly and steadily, to extract the maximum flavor from the beans."

I snuggled under my covers, my fingers wrapped tight around the phone. Who ever knew coffee roasting could sound so sexy?

So that's why, the following Thursday, when James

invited me to roast with him and we didn't have Claudia to worry about, I was utterly tempted. I told him to hang on a second. Then I stepped onto the sidewalk and dialed the home line from my cell phone. The sleet had finally stopped coming down and the air was dry and mild.

V answered on the second ring. "Hello?"

"Hey, it's me."

"What's up?"

"I was thinking about . . . I was thinking I won't get home until a little later. Maybe eleven-forty-five or midnight."

"Bethany again?" V asked.

Was V on to me? I hadn't told her anything about James and, despite that question about my neck splotch, she hadn't done any further prying into whether I was falling in love.

When I didn't respond, V quickly said, "You know that's funny because Bethany called here earlier and said she was panicking about an exam tomorrow and you're the only one who can help her."

What?

V was quiet for a second. I could hear my dad's voice in the background, like he'd just stepped into the room.

"I know, I know," V said as if we were in the middle of a conversation. "I told Bethany you could probably stop by after Common Grounds. Do you want me to let your parents know you'll be home a little late?"

"She didn't really call, did she?"

V didn't respond for several seconds, which I took as a no, and then she said, "Just keep your cell phone on in case anyone needs to reach you. Tell Bethany I said to stay calm."

"You're good at this."

"Lots of practice," V said.

The rest of the night was seamless. My dad didn't even call to check up on me. And when I got home, my parents had already gone to bed. That was a relief because my cheeks were flushed from a quick make-out session in the supply closet and my clothes and hair were impregnated with an intensely smoky coffee scent.

Even so, on Saturday morning, I sent Bethany an e-mail asking if she could talk in person. She wrote me back a few minutes later and said she's home all day if I wanted to stop by. The freezing rain was coming down again, so I put on my raincoat and sneakers. My dad was at his office and V was up in her room. I told my mom I was driving over to Bethany's. It was a relief to actually mean it for once.

Bethany met me at her front door. She was wearing a Geneseo sweatshirt, and her scribbles of hair were held back by a paisley bandanna.

"Does that sweatshirt mean what I think it means?" I asked as I kicked off my soggy sneakers.

Bethany smiled. "The acceptance letter came last week."

"Congatulations!"

Just then, Bethany's mom walked down the hallway

carrying a heaping laundry basket. We chatted colleges and summer plans for a few minutes before Bethany steered me upstairs to her room.

"So what's up?" she asked, closing the door. "Your e-mail sounded mysterious."

I glanced around Bethany's room. I hadn't been over in almost a year. The last time I was here, her walls were plastered with magazine cutouts of pop stars and posters of sleeping kittens with expressions underneath like WAKE ME UP WHEN IT'S SATURDAY. But they were all gone and in their place were volleyball pendants and photos of her with a muscular blond-haired guy.

"I have a confession to make," I said, sitting on her bed. "I've been using you as an alibi. In the last month, we've been going to movies and we've studied together and you've joined the yearbook staff."

"I've always wanted to be on yearbook!" Bethany squealed, flopping down on the bed next to me. "What section did I work on? Did I put in tons of candids of me and all my friends?"

I cracked up. "I'm sorry I didn't tell you before, but—"

"Is he cute?"

"Who?"

Bethany tugged at a loose thread on her quilt. "The guy you've made all these excuses for?"

"Very cute," I said, smiling.

"Do tell."

It felt good to finally talk about James. I told Bethany

how he's twenty-two and has his own apartment and, even though it's only been a month, we're falling in love, though neither of us have said the L-word yet. When she asked how I met him and I said he's the guy who owns Common Grounds, she yanked at the thread so hard she actually pulled it out.

"I know who that is! He's not just cute. He's HOT!"

I grinned. "I think so, too."

"My boyfriend's also in his twenties. Well, he's only twenty."

"That guy in all the pictures?"

Bethany nodded. "It'll be four months on Thursday."

"So . . . ?"

"His name's Keith Sawyer. Isn't that a great name?" Bethany sighed. "Bethany Sawyer. I love that."

So I hadn't been the only one playing the name game. *Mara McCloskey. Mara Elizabeth McCloskey. Mara Valentine-McCloskey. Mara Elizabeth Valentine Herbert McCloskey.*

"He's a sophomore at Geneseo," Bethany said. "He's from Long Island. We met through volleyball. He's the bane of my parents' existence."

"Why?"

"They can't get over the fact that he's twenty, even though I've explained to them a hundred times that when I was fifteen, I went out with guys who were seventeen and that's the same age difference." Bethany tossed the thread onto her rug. "And also . . . well . . . I told them I want to get an apartment with him next year rather than live in the dorms."

"What'd they say?"

"Over their dead bodies."

"What did you say?"

"I asked whether they wanted to be buried or cremated."

"Wow," I said, laughing.

"My mom acted all normal downstairs, but we've been fighting like crazy this week. I can't wait to get out of here and be on my own."

I nodded, wondering if everyone has a hard time with their parents senior year.

Bethany and I chatted for over an hour about our boyfriends and who's gotten into what college. Around noon, her mom called upstairs, something about needing help with the laundry already.

"She's pissed," Bethany said. "I can hear it in her voice. She can't deal with me having any fun right now."

As we hopped off the bed and headed downstairs, I said, "We should hang out sometime."

"For real?" Bethany asked. "Or wink-wink?"

"How about both?"

Bethany laughed. "Do you want to see *Damn Yankees* together? It's the weekend after next."

"Sounds great."

"Did you know that Lindsey's in the chorus?"

I shook my head.

"She can't stop talking about V."

"Good or bad?"

"Omigod . . . great! She says V's a star."

"Really?"

Bethany nodded. "Broadway quality."

Tuesday was April Fool's Day. It was also the last night of V's SAT prep course. They were doing this special session on the college-application process for students and their parents. It wasn't mandatory. And they'd already handed back the final practice SAT, which V rocked to the point where there's a strong chance she'll surpass my score on the actual exam.

V kept saying she didn't see the point in going to the session, especially since she's not even sure she's applying to college. My parents, upon hearing that, tried not to balk too overtly. Instead they calmly said that it couldn't hurt to hear what they have to say and, hey, some colleges have great theater programs. V still wasn't convinced, so they suggested going for half and then taking her out to a steakhouse afterward. V finally agreed, her face brightening at the prospect of a juicy tenderloin.

After they headed to Rochester, I sat at my desk and began writing up a physics lab on the heat of fusion and ice. It's due tomorrow. Generally, I would have finished it already and by this point would just be double-checking the numbers. But lately I've been putting off assignments until the last minute and then turning in dog-eaten excuses for homework. And the crazy thing is that I've still been getting top grades.

I was in the middle of determining the percentage of error when my cell phone rang. I didn't recognize the number on caller ID, but I answered anyway. At first, I could only hear whimpers, so I figured it must be some kind of April Fool's prank. I was about to push the "cancel" button when this muffled voice said, "Mara?"

"Claudia?" I asked. "Are you okay?"

Claudia sniffled and choked. At some point, she said something that sounded like, "Why . . . didn't . . . tell . . . me-e-e-e-e-e?"

"What?"

"Why didn't yo-o-o-o-o-o . . ." Claudia dissolved into sobs again.

I could hear someone taking the phone from her and then this woman's voice said, "Mara?"

"Yeah?"

"This is Pauline. Claudia's roommate."

I'd met Pauline before. She comes into Common Grounds now and then, and Claudia always slips her free cups of coffee. She's got a long freckled nose that's constantly buried in a psychology textbook.

"Hey," I said, "we've actually—"

Pauline cut me off and launched into this story about how Claudia happened to be driving by James's apartment this afternoon and saw a car in the parking lot that looked uncannily like mine. She got out to double-check and, sure enough, there was my bag in the passenger seat.

I was speechless. Yes, I'd been over at James's, but the Presidents Village parking lots are on either side of the apartment complex, off the main road. You don't just *happen* by them. You go in looking.

The whole time Pauline was talking, Claudia was sobbing in the background.

"Can I talk to Claudia?" I asked Pauline.

"I don't think she's up for it."

"Can I at least tell her I'm sorry?"

"*Sorry?* How could you be *sorry?* You have control over your motivations. Don't you know anything about ego and id?"

Ego and id? What did this have to do with ego and id?

"I'm just . . ." I massaged my forehead. "It's just . . . It just happened . . . I didn't mean to hurt—"

"Well, you did. You promised her there was nothing going on. Do you know what it does to someone when you betray their trust? It scars them, okay? We're talking *deep psychological wounds.* But you'll be happy to know that she's resigned from Common Grounds. We just sent an e-mail to James. So now you two can go ahead and cross all those inappropriate boundaries in public and be as pathological as you want."

The last thing Pauline said was, "You need some serious therapy." And then she hung up.

chapter sixteen

Sure enough, V was a star.

On a rainy Friday night in the middle of April, *Damn Yankees* debuted at Brockport High School. I went with Bethany and her boyfriend, Keith. We ended up sitting in the third row of the auditorium, right next to Lindsey Breslawski's brother, Jordan, and their aunt and uncle. My parents were two rows in front of us, my mom with the video camera, my dad with the digital camera. They'd promised to e-mail pictures to Aimee as soon as they got home.

For the past few weeks, Aimee had been a touchy subject around our house. Ever since February, Aimee had been calling on a fairly regular basis. V really wanted her to fly up to Brockport for the *Damn Yankees* weekend. At first, Aimee said she could do it, and my parents even offered to buy the ticket. But then, two weeks ago, she called back to say that things were getting crazy and don't get the plane ticket after all. She never specified what she meant by "crazy," but after my dad relayed the news, V said how Aimee never comes through for anyone and how, mark her words, whenever Aimee says things are "getting crazy," a breakup is about to happen and, mark her words, we're going to get a call from Aimee within the month saying she's decided that her life's ambition is to make cheese in Wisconsin or work on a fishing boat in Alaska.

By the end of V's rant, her face was splotchy. She stormed up to her room. My mom followed her but came back downstairs a minute later and said that V didn't want to talk. For the past few weeks, whenever one of us mentions Aimee, V huffs and says, "Yeah, right" or "Mark my words, a fishing boat in Alaska." After Aimee called this afternoon to tell V to break a leg, V disappeared into her room and didn't come out until it was time for my dad to drive her over to the high school.

But V didn't reveal any of this onstage. When she first swiveled out in the middle of act one, people stopped coughing and picking their wedgies and passing breath mints to friends. The audience froze, their eyes transfixed on her. Some guys, like Jordan Breslawski, actually leaned forward in their chairs, though I had a feeling it was to get a better view of her cleavage.

V was dressed a lot like the movie version of Lola, in a black strapless one-piece—part leotard, part corset—with a flirty ruffle at the hips. She was wearing fishnet stockings and black heels. Her hair had been set in rollers by one of the backstage moms, so her honey curls bounced down her back and her now-grown-out bangs were swept to the side. Another backstage mom had expertly applied her makeup so her cheekbones were pronounced and her lips were sultry. And, then, of course, there was her cleavage.

We'd had a conversation about that the night before. V was getting dropped off from the dress rehearsal at the same time as I was coming home from Common Grounds. As we walked across the driveway, I said her stage makeup looked impressive.

V paused under a yard light. "You want to see impressive?"

She unbuttoned her jacket and cupped her hands beneath the twin peaks that had erupted under her T-shirt. "What do you think? I have ta-tas! Hooters! Knockers!"

"What's in there?"

"A push-up bra and lots of foam. Who ever knew a bra could work such wonders?"

"So you think you'll start wearing a bra now?"

V shrugged. "It's fun for the play, but what's the point? There's not much to hold up anyway."

"Do you ever want . . ." I paused. "Do you ever wish—"

"That Valentine girls weren't denied the boob gene?"

I laughed. "I guess that's one way to put it."

"I like not having to wear a bra. I figure one day, when I'm forty or something, I'll probably start drooping. Maybe I'll wear a bra then. I don't know. I'm in no rush."

But it wasn't just V's va-va-voom appearance that was

capturing all that attention. It was the way she spoke in this cutely seductive voice and tilted her chin to one side and strutted around in her heels, swinging her hips. When she belted out her first number, "A Little Brains, a Little Talent," I actually forgot that the pit band was off-key and we were in the high-school auditorium and V was Lola or Lola was V.

When she finished singing, the audience burst into applause. I could see my dad clapping, his hands raised above his head. My mom turned the video camera toward the audience, to record the response. When she spotted me, I formed the letter V with my pointer and middle finger. As I did, I realized it was the same thing as the peace sign.

The audience finally quieted down when the next scene began. I could see Bethany and Keith reach for each other's hands. It made me wish James were here.

I'd briefly considered inviting him, if it weren't for the fact that my parents would wonder why my boss from Common Grounds was coming to the school play with me. In the past ten days since that phone call from Claudia/Pauline, our relationship had gone to a whole different level. When I look back, it's like we spent our first month kissing and joking around a lot. And while we're still doing that, it now feels like there's a new element to us, a deeper element.

After Pauline hung up on me, I'd called James at Common Grounds. I was crying so hard, I could barely talk.

But I didn't have to explain because he'd just gotten Claudia's e-mail of resignation. He asked if I wanted to meet him somewhere or go to his apartment. I couldn't do anything but sob into the phone. James asked if my parents were home and I choked out a no and he said he was on his way over. Five minutes later, he pulled in the driveway. As I climbed into the passenger seat of his car, he hugged me and rubbed my back until I stopped crying.

"Do you think I'm horrible?" I asked, wiping my cheeks.

James picked up my hand, kissing one finger at a time. "You're not horrible, Mara. You could never be horrible. Maybe we should have talked to Claudia, let her know we were together, but you were just trying to protect her from getting hurt."

"I went behind her back and then I lied to her."

"But don't you think she knew? Don't you think she sensed something was going on? She *drove* into my parking lot."

"But I stole her from you."

"It's not like we were together and I cheated on her with you."

"But she liked you and I'm her friend and friends don't do things like that."

"But Claudia could have been a better friend to you, too. She must have known on some level that I wasn't interested in her in that way. So if she sensed that you and

I liked each other, she shouldn't have held you back from being with me. That's not fair. You can't stand in the way of love."

He said it.

For the first time in the History of Mara and James, someone said it. I looked at James and he looked at me and we sat there, holding hands and looking at each other. And suddenly it felt like despite Claudia and despite our age difference and despite me going away to Yale and despite all the cards that were stacked against us, we were meant to be together.

At the end of the play, the audience gave the cast a standing ovation. When V curtsied, she got thundering applause. As the curtain lowered for the final time, my parents and I headed backstage to bring V the massive bouquet of white roses that my mom had ordered from Arjuna Florist.

V was surrounded by ogling freshmen guys, but we cut through the throng and hugged her and told her what a great job she did. Her eyes got teary as she thanked us for sticking by her and encouraging her to go for it.

My dad snapped pictures of V with members of the cast. My mom chatted with Lindsey's aunt. I scanned the faces backstage to see who I knew, waving at various kids. And then I turned my head and saw Dr. Hendrick.

He was standing about fifteen feet from me, shaking hands with Mr. B. I was tempted to walk over and tell him off once and for all. I wanted to say that he shouldn't have dissed me at that play rehearsal and it was the best thing I'd ever done to drop his stupid class.

But then I remembered how he'd choreographed all of V's dances and had really helped her shine. As I thought about that, I didn't feel as angry at him. It wasn't about me right now. What mattered was V. This was her moment.

Once V had scrubbed her face with cold cream and changed into jeans and signed the programs of three wide-eyed middle schoolers, we piled into Keith's car and drove up to Friendly's. Most of the cast was already there, several of them still decked out in their poodle skirts and base-ball uniforms. They all waved V toward their tables, but she gestured that she was going to sit with us.

We settled into a booth, Bethany and Keith on one side, V and me on the other side. We chatted about who forgot a line and who tripped onstage and who surprised us with their hidden talent. Keith didn't say much, just little comments now and then. But you could tell he was sweet, the way he kept gazing at Bethany and stroking her arm.

When the waitress came over, Bethany ordered mint-chip ice cream with extra hot fudge. Keith ordered onion rings and a Coke. V ordered a malted milk shake. I was about to order my usual, raspberry sorbet, when I glanced down at the menu and said, "I'd like a grilled-cheese sandwich."

"Cheddar or Swiss?" the waitress asked.

"Can I get both?"

The waitress scribbled something on her pad and took our menus. As she headed toward the kitchen, V gaped at me. "Am I crazy or did you just order an animal byproduct?"

"I guess I'm craving cheese."

"Next thing you know you'll be craving hamburgers," V said. "The late, great vegan eating juicy burgers."

That's the kind of thing that used to piss me off about V, but it didn't bother me now. I could tell she was just kidding around.

"Mmmmm," I said, licking my lips, "with crispy bacon on top."

"Are you *serious?*" V asked. "You're really craving *bacon?*"

I shook my head. "Gotcha!"

"Ha! You totally had me there."

Bethany and Keith were staring at us like they had no idea what we were talking about.

"You guys," Bethany finally said, "are *so incredibly* related."

V smiled at me. I smiled back at her, thinking how I didn't take that as an insult, not even for a second.

chapter seventeen

My parents decided to take V to New York City to see a Broadway musical. Partially, it was because they were proud of her performance as Lola, so they wanted to do something special for her. And partially because there was a teachers' conference on a Monday at the end of April, so school was closed for a long weekend. And partially because their friend, Mike Shreves, was having a birthday bash in Manhattan that Saturday night, so my parents said it would be a good excuse to go.

But I know my parents well enough to know that there are *always* hidden motives, especially in the spring of junior year. Lo and behold, my parents did not disappoint. Once V had said yes and my mom had purchased three tickets to *Hairspray,* they mentioned that, hey, it couldn't hurt to go on a tour of NYU. After all, they have Tisch School of the Arts, which is one of the most prestigious undergraduate acting programs in the country. And then, a few days later, they said that rather than flying down on JetBlue, why don't they take off Friday as well and drive to the city? The weather is mild and, besides, they can meander by Hamilton and Bard and Colgate on the way back and check out the campuses.

I'd been invited to join them, but I said that my statistics final was coming up and senior-class council was consuming the rest of my time as prom preparations kicked into high gear.

LIE! LIE! LIE!

My Big and Illicit Reason for not going was that I wanted to spend the night with James. Over the past few weeks, things were really heating up with us. We'd started fooling around on his bed and he'd been touching inside my bra and sometimes even kissing there. One time, when he was doing that, I pulled up his T-shirt, too, and pressed my chest against his chest. That felt so good that whenever I thought about it, I'd smile uncontrollably, even if I was sitting in physics or pushing back my cuticles or waiting at a stoplight.

But despite all of this, I felt like there was this constant time pressure with James and me. We had an hour, a half hour, my cell phone might ring, he had to be back at Common Grounds. We always had to be ready to wash our faces and gather our hair into ponytails and think of an excuse for where I was.

So when my parents mentioned leaving town and taking V with them, it was like a light-bulb-over-the-head

176

solution. I talked about it with James and we came to the conclusion that I couldn't sleep at his apartment because my parents might call our house late at night to make sure I'm there. But we *could* pull off having James sleep at my place. If my parents called, I could just be like, *Sure, don't worry about me, everything's fine.*

And so, on Friday morning, I helped them load the car with munchies and maps and dressy clothing in dry-cleaner bags. As my mom backed down the driveway, my dad told me to leave my cell phone on and always lock the doors.

"I will," I said.

V leaned out her window. "Don't do anything I wouldn't do!"

I considered that for a second. There's probably not much that V wouldn't do, so I waved and shouted, "I won't!"

They all waved back and my mom drove down our street. I watched as the Yale bumper sticker got farther and farther away and then was out of sight.

As it turned out, James had to go to Schenectady on Friday night for his grandmother's ninetieth birthday party. It's a four-hour drive, so he was going to sleep over and return the following afternoon. That evening, I went to a movie with Bethany and Lindsey, got home by ten-thirty, called my parents, and then went to bed. As I lay under my covers, I couldn't stop thinking about how James was going to sleep over the next night. I ran my hand over my hips, slipping my fingers inside the elastic band of my underwear. Sometimes, when James and I are kissing and I'm pressing my body against him, I have this urge for him to touch me down there.

I was restless the whole next day. I spent forty-five minutes distractedly flipping through the Johns Hopkins course catalog. Even though I don't have to register for my summer classes until the end of May, my parents keep bugging me to do it sooner rather than later so I can be sure to get my first choices. But I can't seem to figure out what I want to take. Whenever I think about this summer, I think how I'd rather be spending my last two months before college with James, not pressure-cooking in some classroom in Baltimore.

I set the course catalog aside and sent some e-mails to various members of the senior-class council about the prom budget. I mined the cupboards for snack foods and left a message with Bethany and opened and closed *Elementary Statistics.* I took a shower and shaved my legs. I rubbed my mom's expensive skin cream all over my body. I resisted squeezing a few blackheads on my chin because I didn't want them to be swollen that night.

Finally, I put on my sneakers and walked to the canal. I made a serious attempt along the way to appreciate the yellow daffodils and newly budding trees. But all I could think about was that James would be back in a few hours, we'd work together at Common Grounds, he'd come over to my house, and then . . .

OH. MY. FREAKING. GOD.

James and I would sleep in the same bed tonight!

That evening, James and I kept smiling at each other and bumping hips and drawing hearts on receipt tape. It didn't help that he wore his faded jeans with the hole in the thigh. And it didn't help that it was warm and balmy, a perfect spring night. And it didn't help that my coworker Josh kept singing "Love Is in the Air."

After Claudia quit, James reorganized the schedule to cover her shifts. He decided to separate Josh and Randy, since the two of them together upped the loud ante to a near-deafening pitch. When Josh joined my shifts, we didn't overtly tell him we were together, but we didn't hide our affection, either, so he'd pretty much guessed it by now.

But Josh was right about Saturday night. There was definitely a feeling in the air, some blend of love and excitement and anticipation.

Things got even more exciting as the evening progressed. The chubby older woman/skinny younger guy were sitting at their regular table, drinking their regular decaf cappuccinos and sharing their regular piece of blueberry cheesecake. They've been in here almost every weekend since January, when Claudia and I presumed they met on the Internet. They're always nuzzling and holding hands. I used to think they were a bizarre mismatch, how she's practically double his age and he's practically half her size. But over the past few months, I've gotten used to them.

Around nine-thirty, I was unloading mugs from the dishwasher. James was filling a jar with chocolate-covered espresso beans. Josh was singing, "Love is in the air, love is in the air, oh, oh, oh, oh, uh, uh, uh, uh . . ."

Just as Josh hit his last "uh" and I stacked my last mug, the skinny guy rose out of his chair, knelt down on one knee, and held out a little jewelry box. The woman slowly set down her forkful of cheesecake. I tapped James's elbow and pointed in their direction. As soon as he realized what was happening, he turned to Josh and said, *"Shhhhhhhhhhhhhhh!"*

Everyone in Common Grounds was staring at them. The guy was still kneeling. The woman nodded as she looked into the now-open box. He slipped the ring on the fourth finger of her left hand and they started hugging and kissing. Everyone applauded. I could feel myself tearing up.

"SEE???" Josh shouted, stretching his arms out to either side. "LOVE IS IN THE AIR!"

James clapped his hands together and made an announcement that decaf cappuccinos and slices of blueberry cheesecake were on the house.

More applause.

As I began making cappuccinos and Josh, who had resumed his singing, served up the cheesecake, I got this sad feeling in my throat. I was thinking about Claudia and how, when the now-engaged couple first came into Common Grounds, I'd joked that the woman wanted a "bling-bling on her fing-fing." Claudia would have gotten a kick out of being here tonight and seeing my prediction come true.

Once the line of freebie seekers eased up, I told James I was taking a quick break. I stepped onto the sidewalk and pulled my cell phone out of my pocket. I clicked through until I got to Claudia's number.

Unfortunately, Pauline answered.

"Is Claudia there?" I asked.

"May I ask who's calling?"

"It's Mara."

"Mara from Common Grounds?"

"Yeah."

Pauline cleared her throat. "I thought you understood that Claudia doesn't want to talk to you."

"But I thought—"

"Don't you know about Pavlov's dogs?"

"What?" I asked. "Whose dogs?"

"Pavlov's. It was a psychological experiment where the dogs' mouths salivated whenever Pavlov rang a bell because they thought they were going to get fed."

"I'm not sure what this has to do with—"

"That's called a 'conditioned response,'" Pauline said.

"And you should be conditioned to know that if you ring here, guess what response you're going to get?"

"What?"

"Goodbye," Pauline said, hanging up.

I slid my phone back into my pocket. I felt like crying. I really needed to talk to Claudia, to tell her I was sorry for going behind her back, to hear that maybe, just maybe, she was willing to forgive me.

I pulled out my phone again and dialed V's cell.

"Mara?" she asked. I could hear voices and laughing and silverware clinking.

"Where are you?"

"What?"

"I said, 'Where are you?'"

"It's too loud in here. Hold on."

I could hear V saying something and then my dad saying, "What's wrong? Is Mara okay?" and V saying, "Yeah, I think she just called to say hi."

A minute later, V breathlessly said, "Hey, there! I just ran out to the sidewalk."

"Where are you?"

"We're at that birthday party for your parents' friends. It's a totally fancy restaurant, but get this . . . They don't even serve ketchup! *Ketchup?* Can you imagine a restaurant not having ketchup?"

I laughed. "How's it going otherwise?"

"Oh, fine. We're going to *Hairspray* tomorrow night.

And we saw NYU this afternoon. G-ma and G-pa are convinced that it's the school for me."

"What do you think?"

"We'll see. So how're you? What's up?"

"This is probably going to sound completely out of the blue." I paused for a moment. "I just wanted to say I'm sorry I was so hard on you . . . about what happened with you and Travis."

V didn't say anything. The light changed on Main Street and several cars whizzed by.

"V? Did you hear me?"

"Yeah," she said quietly.

"Did I totally weird you out?"

"No . . . I'm just thinking . . ." V trailed off. "I'm just thinking . . . you don't know how badly I needed to hear that."

"Really?"

"It was a shitty thing to do. I don't know why I'm such an idiot all the time."

"No, you're not."

"Well, sometimes."

"We all do stupid things sometimes. But that doesn't mean—"

"Not you," V said.

Not me?! I'm a Pavlovian dog, a traitorous inflicter of deep psychological wounds.

"Yes, me," I said. "Definitely me."

• • •

At first, it was weird being with James at my house. He'd never been inside before, so I felt kind of nervous. Not in a hostessy way, like I had to dote on him, and not even in a guilty way, like I thought I was going to get caught. My parents were definitely, positively in New York City. And I'd driven James over from Common Grounds, so neighbors wouldn't see both of our cars pulling in the driveway.

I think the nerves were coming more from the collision of two worlds. My parents' house, my report card on the fridge, my childhood. And then James, that sexy smile on his face, that hole in his jeans, the me who I am now.

I dealt with it by fluttering all over, asking James if he wanted anything to eat (no), if he wanted water (yes), if he wanted ice in his water (no), if he wanted to brush his teeth (maybe later). When I told him how we had extra toothbrushes, he laughed and said he wouldn't expect less in a dentist's house.

I gave him a quick tour. We ended up in my bedroom. James glanced at the framed photos of me with my family and then started looking through my bookshelf. I picked up the phone to call my parents. I decided to dial my mom's cell since she's less likely to answer. When I got her voice mail, I said I'm home (true) and going to sleep (false), so tell Dad not to worry and I'd talk to them tomorrow.

When I hung up, James said, "Wow."

I shifted my makeup box so it was aligned with the corner of my dresser. "Wow, I'm becoming an expert liar?"

"Wow, you've organized your books in alphabetical order by author."

"I like to be able to find everything. What's wrong with that?"

James set his glass on a coaster on my desk and came up behind me, wrapping his arms around my waist. "Nothing's wrong with it . . . I love that about you."

"You do?"

He kissed the back of my neck. "I love seeing how you do things."

"And you approve?"

"Of course I approve."

We kissed for a while in the middle of my room. At one point, I glanced into the mirror above my dresser. It was weird to see myself, gangly and flushed, stooping toward James. I reached over and turned off the overhead light. As I did, James took my hand and led me to the bed.

I only have a twin bed, so we squished together on top of the blanket. After a while, James reached under my shirt. But rather than pushing my shirt up in the front like I usually do, I wriggled it over my head and then took off my bra.

"You're so beautiful," James whispered.

"You can't see me. It's completely dark in here."

"Well, I can feel you and you feel beautiful."

I kissed James's neck and ran my hands along his shoulders. Then I pulled up his shirt. He helped me take it all the way off. As he wrapped his arms around me, I was so drunk with the sensation of skin on skin I could hardly breathe.

"I love you, James," I whispered.

"I love you, too."

We started kissing again. We were both wearing jeans, but I could feel through our layers that he was hard between his legs. I pressed myself against him and we moved our hips together, slowly at first and then faster and faster.

We were still kissing and my hips were rotating and my heart was racing and there was this incredible energy in my whole body, like I could do this forever and ever and ever. But then a surging sensation spread to my arms and legs and fingers and toes, leaving me warm and breathless.

As James stroked my hair, I pressed my face into his neck, closed my eyes, and smiled into the darkness.

chapter eighteen

Three weeks later, my homeroom teacher sent me to Mr. B's office. I was talking with Mindy Vance, the girl who sits behind me, about the music for the prom. She'd heard we'd hired a DJ from Rochester and was nervous that the songs would be "all loud and *urban.*" She spat out "urban" like it was a bitter salad green. I reassured her that there would definitely be recognizable songs. Not necessarily the chicken dance, but the prom theme is "End of the Road," so it's not like we're going to get too obscure.

"Mara Valentine?" my homeroom teacher called out.

I glanced toward the front of the room. Mr. Flowers always uses my last name even though there are no other Maras in my homeroom, and for David Vandusen and David Wolk he just says *David* and then points to the one he wants. It's almost like Mr. Flowers has decided that he's endured enough taunts about *his* last name, so why not inflict that on someone else?

"The vice principal sent a note up here," Mr. Flowers said. "He wants you to report to the main office after homeroom."

"Do you know why?"

Mr. Flowers shook his head.

When the bell rang, I headed downstairs. I must have been completely spaced out because I couldn't figure out why Mr. B wanted to see me. But when I walked into the main office and Rosemary, smiling her Cheshire grin, escorted me to Mr. B's door and I saw Travis Hart sitting in one of the chairs, it hit me:

This was it.

The final score had been tallied and, forever in history or at least on a plaque on the wall outside the main office, one of us was going to be first and one of us was going to be second.

"Have a seat," Rosemary said. "Mr. B will be right in."

As I sat in the other chair, Travis nodded ever so slightly in my direction. His long legs were sprawled out at a ninety-degree angle and his elbows were rammed into the armrests. He was massaging his temples with his thumbs, his fingers interlaced across his forehead.

The glass bowl on Mr. B's desk was full of M&M's. I pinched up three greens. Ever since that grilled-cheese sandwich at Friendly's, I've been eating dairy again, which of course includes chocolate. I've even allowed myself "hidden eggs" like in cookies and muffins.

Mr. B appeared in the doorway. His long strands of

hair still revealed the comb grooves, like a recently plowed field.

"Hello, Travis! Hello, Mara!" he exclaimed, patting us both on the shoulder as he made his way to his desk.

Mr. B sat down in his chair and clasped his hands together, resting them on his Pooh-Bear belly. "I imagine you both know why you're here."

I nodded. Travis flinched.

Mr. B began twiddling his thumbs together, like he was having a thumbie war with himself. And then he launched into a *loooooong* monologue that included several words like *exemplary* and at least three mentions of torch carrying.

As he talked, Travis's face got redder and redder. Just as he was saying something about how grades are just numbers, not judges of character, Travis said, "Okay, okay. We're both great, everything's great, now who got it, me or Mara?"

"Well," Mr. B said, "I wanted to preface myself because your final grade-point averages were so close, only two-tenths of a point apart . . ."

Travis let out this throaty groan.

"But I guess I'll cut to the chase." Mr. B pinned one of his thumbs down with the other. "Mara got it. Mara came in ahead. She's our valedictorian."

"God *damn!*" Travis said, punching his fist into the armrest.

Mr. B's smile slid off his face. "Travis, you are still our salutatorian. You'll still be making the thirty-second—"

"Concession speech."

"We like to call it the salutatory address."

"Whatever," Travis said, standing up. "Can I get out of here?"

But Travis didn't even wait for a response. He took off, leaving Mr. B and me staring at the empty doorway.

"I've never seen Travis Hart behave like that," Mr. B said, shaking his head.

I have, I thought. That's exactly how Travis used to act when we were together. When I told him that my jeans were remaining zipped, he'd say things like, "Sucks for me." Back then, I thought it was my fault, that I had a major character defect. But since I've been with James and discovered how good things can be, I've realized that Travis is a temper-tantrum-throwing bully. I don't even find him attractive anymore. His shaved head looks too puny for his body and his "charming" smile seems fake and his "easygoing" strut seems forced.

Mr. B crunched on a few M&M's and told me how my valedictory address should run three to four minutes and that he had sample speeches in his files, if I wanted to peruse them.

As he walked me to the door, he shook my hand. "So . . . how do you feel?"

I shrugged.

"Too happy for words?"

"I guess," I said.

But what I was really thinking was that, strangely, I didn't feel anything.

My parents were definitely feeling something. That night, they made a huge celebratory dinner. Pasta primavera, French bread, salad with marinated artichokes on top. They even opened the bottle of champagne that's been in our fridge since New Year's Eve and let V and me have a little glass. All through the meal, they kept saying, "Congratulations!" and "To our valedictorian!" Or one of them would ask, "Can you believe it?" and the other would nod and say, "Yes, of course I can!"

V didn't say much. She sipped her champagne and picked the pasta out of the primavera and, every once in a while, touched her hands to her hair. Yesterday my mom took her to a salon in Rochester. The stylist brought up the back and blended in her bangs with the sides, so her haircut looks really striking, especially with her high forehead and long neck. My mom offered to take me, too, but I opted out. My hair is finally long enough that it'll all stay in a ponytail, which means I don't have to blow-dry it every day if I don't want to.

I didn't say much during dinner, either. Partially, my head was woozy from the champagne. But it was more that I wasn't sure how I felt about the whole valedictorian thing. For all of high school, I'd been looking at it as this end-all-be-all Final Chapter of the Book of My Life. But now that I've flipped to the last page, there's no music swelling, no credits rolling, no tingly happiness. To be perfectly honest, it still didn't feel like much of anything.

After dinner, my parents insisted on doing the dishes. I carried my plate into the kitchen and said, "I'm going to take a walk."

"Want company?" V asked.

"Sure."

It was a warm May night, so we slipped our feet into flip-flops and headed out the back door. I was wearing a tank top and khaki shorts. V had on her mutilated jeans and a lavender T-shirt.

V and I walked down the driveway, crossed the street, and took a left. We headed to the end of the block, our flip-flops slapping against the sidewalk. There were no cars at the intersection, so we crossed diagonally to the path that runs along the periphery of the school district.

"Are you excited?" V asked as she picked up a long stick from the side of the path.

"About getting valedictorian?"

"Yeah."

"I don't know. . . . It still feels kind of weird."

V was trailing the stick behind her, like she was pulling a wheelie suitcase. "Well, *I'm* really happy for you."

"Thanks."

"It's funny . . . My whole life, I've always heard all these great things about you. Like whenever I screwed up, Aimee would hold you up as this example of what I should be. *Mara* is a straight-A student. *Mara* got honor roll. *Mara* got into Yale. Don't take this the wrong way, but you weren't exactly easy to like."

"No . . . it's okay," I said. And I meant it. It's not like I've been her lifelong fan, either.

"I'm just saying that I used to be so jealous of everything you had. Your grades and your parents and how you seemed like this perfect person. But ever since I was in *Damn Yankees,* I just feel like I have my thing and you have yours."

We were nearing the Barclay School, where I went to second and third grade. We crossed the street and headed over to the huge playground that spans the lawns between the elementary schools. V was now clutching her stick in her fist, like a wizard's staff.

"That's one of the reasons I've been meaning to thank you," she said.

"Thank *me?*"

"For not telling your parents about my smoking habits."

"You mean the noncigarette variety?"

V nodded. "It's something I got into in San Diego, but I've been cutting back a lot recently. I haven't touched it since before the play. I'm just glad G-ma and G-pa never found out. Sometimes you need to have people who only see the good in you."

We walked by an empty row of teeter-totters, half teetering, half tottering.

"Well, thank you, too, then," I said.

193

"Me? Why?"

"For not telling my parents about . . . about how I've been falling in love."

V stopped walking and turned to me. "So I was right?"

I smiled. "Yeah . . . you were right."

"Who is it? I'm assuming it's not Bethany because she's together with Keith . . . hold on!" V stabbed her stick into the grass. "It's the guy from Common Grounds! James, right?"

I stared at her. "How did you know?"

"Remember how you didn't want me to work at Common Grounds because you said it was your place?"

I nodded.

"And remember that time when you were sick and he called and you didn't want to talk to him?"

I nodded again.

"Being Aimee's daughter," V said, "you get pretty good at detecting when there's something going on."

As we started walking again, V asked, "Is it serious?"

"Yeah," I said warily.

"Don't worry," she said. "I'm not going to ask if you've done it yet."

I had to laugh.

We reached the tall swings. I sat down on one and pushed with my feet. V flopped onto the one next to me and scratched her stick into the gravel. As I swung past her, I glanced down to see what she was writing. I was surprised to see the words *RIP Stonah Babe.*

"Hey! That's just like . . ."

"Just like what?" V asked.

"Never mind," I said.

"You mean the graffiti on the bathroom walls at school?"

"You've seen it?"

"Of course I've seen it," V said. "I wrote it."

I scuffed my flip-flops into the gravel until my swing came to a stop. "You *what?*"

"That's what some kids in San Diego called me. *Stonah babe.*"

"What about *skanky ho?*"

V laughed as she tossed her stick into the grass. "Nope . . . never been called that. But you have to admit, it's pretty funny."

"Okay, I'm totally confused. *You* wrote all that graffiti?"

V twisted around in her swing several times and then let go, spinning and spinning and spinning. Finally, when she stopped, she said, "You're probably going to think this is totally fucked up, but I've done that whenever I've started at a new school."

"You write things about yourself on bathroom walls?"

V nodded.

"I don't understand."

"You've never been the new kid. I have . . . almost twenty times. And I've learned that if you just go with the flow, everyone ignores you and life sucks. But if you make yourself *known,* even for bad stuff, at least things get interesting and guys flirt with you and stoners invite you

195

to hang out with them. Sometimes it backfires and people give you hell, but you won't be there forever, so it doesn't really matter."

"How did it work out here?"

"At first, it was fine. Same as usual. But then I got into the play and things started changing. And then someone went around and scribbled out all the graffiti."

"That would be me."

V gaped at me. "*You* were the one? Why?"

I shook my head. We started swinging slowly, kicking our heels into the gravel.

"Sometimes it's scary," V said after a moment.

"What?"

"Having a good reputation. Like once you start doing things well, everyone expects more from you."

I nodded, thinking basically about my whole life.

"But I guess it's better than no one expecting anything at all," V said.

Actually, I thought, *that sounds very tempting.*

After a minute I asked, "Do you ever think about Baxter?"

"Baxter Valentine?"

"Yeah . . . how he makes all those animal noises, like he doesn't even care that everyone thinks he's a freak. It just seems kind of liberating."

V laughed. "I can honestly say I've never envied Baxter."

She started pumping her legs, getting some serious elevation. It took me several kicks to catch up with her, but soon we were knee and knee, elbow and elbow. V looked over at me, this maniacal grin on her face, and went, "Woof!"

I laughed so hard I had to clutch the chains to keep from falling off my swing. But when I caught back up with her, I went, "Moooooo!"

"Cock-a-doodle-doooooooo!" she screamed.

"Meeooooooooooooow!"

"Hee-haaaaw! Hee-haaaaw!"

As we heaved our bodies forward and bellowed a barnyard of noises, I never once looked around to see if anyone else was in the playground. It was wildly fun, not to mention the most insane thing I've ever done in my life.

chapter nineteen

The following Saturday, V took the SATs and I dropped out of the Johns Hopkins precollege summer program. It had been building up for a while. First of all, I could never seem to pick my classes. And then, once the weather warmed up, all the seniors began counting down until graduation. But I was having a converse reaction. For me, time couldn't go slowly enough. Every day that passed was a day closer to when I had to say goodbye to James.

The previous week, I'd e-mailed the director of the summer program, asking if I could have a few extra days to send in my course selections. An hour later, I got an e-mail from her assistant, Thomas, saying I could have another week. Before I could stop myself, I wrote back to him and asked what would happen if I dropped out. Two minutes later, a message popped into my box, saying that if I let them know by June fifth, I'd get a 90 percent refund on my tuition.

So there it was. My get-out-of-jail-almost-free card.

I drove V over to the high school for the SATs. It was a sunny morning and she had said she wanted to walk, so my parents plied her with a hearty breakfast, wished her luck, and headed up to Wegmans to do a big shop. But as soon as they were gone, V ran into the bathroom, clutching her stomach.

"Are you okay?" I said, standing outside the closed door.

"I feel nauseous," she said in this small voice.

"Want some water?"

"No . . . I'll be okay."

When she came out of the bathroom ten minutes later, she was still pale. She glanced at the clock. "I'd better get going . . . I don't have a lot of time now."

"Want me to drive you?" I asked.

"Do you mind?"

"No . . . not at all."

We didn't say much on the car ride over. I tried to get V talking about non-SAT-related things, but she just stared out the window. We were trapped behind a slow-moving tractor, so I looked at the red and yellow tulips, thinking how they've come later than usual this year. V was massaging her stomach with her right hand. On her left hand, I noticed she'd written *relax, relax, relax, relax* down each finger and then on her thumb, it said *VVV.*

"You're going to be fine," I said.

She nodded absentmindedly.

"Think how well you did in the practice tests."

"But this is the real thing."

"You can always retake the SATs in the fall if you're not happy with your score."

"But everything goes on my record, so it's better if I do well the first time around."

I looked over at V. She was sounding scarily like me and I don't necessarily mean that in a good way.

After I dropped her off, I called James from my cell phone and asked if he wanted to go to Northampton Park. That's a park outside of Brockport with picnic areas and sledding hills and hiking trails. He said he'd taken the morning off from Common Grounds to do his laundry but was currently standing in front of his window, staring at the cloudless sky. I told him I'd be right over.

It was still early, so Northampton Park was relatively empty. I pulled into a parking lot, locked the car, and we held hands as we walked down this narrow horse trail. After a few minutes, James pointed out a little meadow, almost completely hidden by trees.

"Want to go in?" he asked.

"Okay," I said, stepping off the trail.

We lay in the poky grass for several minutes, looking up at the infinite sky, my head resting on his shoulder. The sun was getting hot, so I lifted up my shirt and tucked it into the bottom of my bra.

"I feel like we're camping," James said.

"I know. . . . It's so quiet."

"Wouldn't it be fun to go camping this summer? Just you and me, somewhere in the Adirondacks."

"I wish."

"I know . . . I keep trying to pretend you're not leaving."

"What if I didn't go?"

James turned his face toward me. "Not go to Johns Hopkins?"

I nodded.

"But haven't you already matriculated?"

I told James how they could refund most of the tuition and I'd pay my parents the difference with money I'd saved from working at Common Grounds.

"You haven't talked about this with your parents?"

"Not yet." Then I laughed and said, "If I dropped out, I'd obviously have to tell them before we packed the car for Baltimore."

James was quiet for a moment. "What made you change your mind?"

"I just don't see why I've been so hung up on entering college as a second-year student. What's the rush to skip over my freshman year?" I snuggled closer to him. "And, besides . . . I want to spend the summer together."

James leaned down and kissed my stomach, now toasty from the sunshine. "Mara Elizabeth," he said, "I would love nothing more than that, but you have to do what feels best for you."

We started kissing. After a few minutes, I rolled over,

so I was on top of him. He held on to my hips and we started moving our bodies together and I thought, *This is what feels best for me. Not in a year, not in ten years, but right here, right now, right in this moment.*

Later that afternoon, I wrote an e-mail to Thomas at Johns Hopkins saying I was sorry but I wasn't going to be attending summer school after all.

Then I clicked "send" and bought back two months of my life.

chapter twenty

Senior year was winding down. Even though teachers were continually expressing the importance of final-exam preparation, everyone knew that GPAs had already been tallied, so nothing we did now mattered in the slightest. In the hallways and even in classes, there were only five subjects that seniors were concentrating on:

1. The prom, in the broad sense, like who's going with whom and where people bought their dresses.
2. The prom, in the narrow sense, like who's going with whom but is *really* hoping to hook up with a different whom.
3. Partying *before* the prom.
4. Partying *after* the prom.
5. Graduation parties and other reasons to drink this summer.

Despite the dozens of hours I'd put into planning "End of the Road," I wasn't going to go. The only person

I wanted to dance with was James, and I couldn't imagine dragging him to a high-school prom. V actually got two invitations—from Brandon Parker and T.J. Zuckerman—and turned them both down. She later told me that Brandon would just want to get stoned the whole time and T.J. had been trying to find an excuse to sleep with her since *Damn Yankees,* and, truthfully, she'd rather stay home and watch a movie.

I spent the morning of the prom decorating the ballroom at the college with streamers and balloons and handpainted road signs, courtesy of the Art Club. Bethany went to the prom with Keith. When I called her the next day to ask how it went, she said the only big news was that Ash and Travis both ditched their dates and made out under the MERGE sign for the entire evening. Bethany said that despite the extreme public display of affection, it was a relief to have Ash doing something other than gossiping about everyone else's business.

A week after the prom, "Breaking Out" arrived at the high school in a massive shipment of boxes. We had a celebratory pizza party in the yearbook office. I ate two slices, a cheese and a veggie supreme, and savored every single bite. We passed around our yearbooks and a bunch of pens. Everyone wanted me to sign on the "Class Personalities" page where Travis and I were voted "Most Likely to Succeed" because, as they said, my signature might be worth cash someday.

It was weird, the whole "Most Likely to Succeed" thing. I remember being thrilled about it last fall, when Travis and I posed for the camera. He clutched a massive wad of Monopoly money, and I held up a piece of paper that said NEXT STOP, OVAL OFFICE. But recently I've been rethinking my notions of success. Like, just because I know how to write an A paper and I'm good at standardized testing, does that make me successful? What about James? According to the unspoken-but-obvious criteria of "Most Likely to Succeed," he's a big failure because he stayed in Brockport and never went to college. But, on the other hand, he owns a profitable business and he's happy, so shouldn't he be considered successful, too?

These questions had been on my mind a lot, which is probably why I was struggling so much with my valedictory address. Every time I sat down at my computer to write an opening line, I could only muster up the cheesiest of clichés like "We've known each other for so long, it's hard to believe we're about to say goodbye . . ." and "As I stand in front of you today, I can see how bright our futures are going to be . . ." When I complained about this to James, he laughed and said, "I have only three words of advice: No Robert Frost."

"What do you mean?"

"Don't say that two roads diverged in a wood and you took the one less traveled . . ."

"What's wrong with that?"

"You will be in the high-school gym, not a yellow wood, and besides, it'll make people resent you."

"Okay," I said. "So do you have any suggestions?"

"Nothing comes to mind."

Mr. B wasn't much help, either. Whenever I saw him in the hall, he'd wave me over and shake my hand and tell me how graduation is his favorite day of the year. Then he'd make me copy down some slogan that he thought would be *perfect* for my speech, such as "Keep your feet on the ground and reach for the stars" or "A mind is like a parachute; it only works when it's open." I actually liked the parachute quote, though I couldn't figure out how to tie jumping out of a plane into a valedictory address.

My parents were definitely more hyped about graduation than I was. It was scheduled for a Friday morning, the third week in June, and they'd both taken off that entire day from work. They'd ordered graduation announcements. And my mom took me shopping at Marketplace Mall for a dress to wear to graduation. We had a fun time together, identifying the various species of mall rats, like preteens on the make and fat guys eating their way through the food court. Things only got awkward when we walked by the Gap and she offered to buy me some clothes for Johns Hopkins. Since I still hadn't told my parents about dropping out, I quickly mumbled, "Maybe another time."

I still hadn't told them about James, either. Sometimes,

like when my mom and I were driving home from the mall, I had this impulse to blurt it out. I almost felt like she'd understand, maybe even be happy for me. But then there was the problem of my dad. She'd obviously have to tell him and, truthfully, I had no idea how he'd react.

V had sworn to keep my secret about James. Every once in a while, she'd ask me how it was going and I'd tell her *fine* and she'd say *great* and that would be that. She actually hadn't been around the house a lot recently. She'd auditioned for a summer community production of *Angels in America* and got cast as Harper, the Valium-addicted young wife, which I thought was ironic given the fact that she was trying to cut back on her own recreational drug habits. So most evenings, she was at rehearsal. And when she wasn't there, she was begging my dad to take her driving.

Over Memorial Day weekend, my parents had taken her to the DMV to get a learner's permit. She and my dad were constantly cruising around town, practicing three-point turns. Whenever V pulled into the driveway, she'd honk triumphantly and flash the headlights on and off. One evening at dinner, my parents reminisced about how when Aimee was learning to drive, she'd squirt a stream of windshield-wiper fluid whenever she accomplished a parallel park.

That night, my mom pulled out the photo albums from Aimee's high-school days. V and I sat with her on the couch. V asked my mom about Aimee's road test and

Aimee's first summer job and Aimee's senior prom. She didn't even sound bitter, like she usually does when the subject of her mom comes up.

Three days later, V got suspended for the rest of the school year.

It all started with a phone call from Aimee. My parents and I were at a National Honor Society banquet when she called. I won awards for service to the school and top grades in government and top grades in physics and top overall GPA. Every time I sat down after receiving another award, one of them would lean over and whisper, "We're so proud of you!"

When we got home, the TV was blaring at full volume and V was slumped on the couch. Her eyes were bloodshot, like she'd been crying, and she was aggressively chewing her fingernails.

"What's wrong?" my dad asked.

V bit her bottom lip and muted the volume with the remote control.

"What is it, sweetie?" my mom asked.

"Aimee called," V finally said. "She's moving to Florida. She wants to learn about the orange-juice business, and she knows someone who can get her a job working at a grove."

"Florida?" my dad asked.

"The orange-juice business?" my mom asked.

"The *fucking* orange-juice business," V said. "She said I

should finish the school year in Brockport and she'll get me a ticket to fly down to Florida as soon as finals are over."

"Did you tell her about *Angels in America?*" my mom asked.

"Yeah . . . she said I can stay through that."

"Well, that's good news," my dad said.

"I don't want to live on a *fucking* orange grove. And, besides, Ms. Green told me that the drama club is going to put on *Chicago* next year and I'm a shoe-in for Roxie."

My parents exchanged a quick glance. No one had said it out loud, but I know they wanted V to stay on with them next year, through the college-application process. It was almost like they'd been crossing their fingers that things would work out for Aimee in Costa Rica and it wouldn't even become an issue.

"Maybe I can talk to Aimee," my dad said. "I'm sure she'll understand if—"

"Understand, my ass," V said. "Aimee doesn't even *like* orange juice. She drinks grapefruit juice. This is *fucking* insane."

Then V blasted the volume on the TV again.

The next day, Ash found me after fourth period. I was at my locker, dropping off my books and getting my car keys and thinking how I'd call James on the way to the student parking lot and see if he wanted to drive to Northampton Park. We'd been back to that meadow several times in the past few weeks and no one else is ever there.

"Hey, Mara."

As soon as I saw Ash, I knew it must be sizzling-hot gossip because she'd been avoiding me since she kissed Travis at the prom.

"Did you hear?" Ash asked.

"Hear what?"

"How V got kicked out of school."

"*What?*"

Ash's lips flickered ever so slightly into a smile. "She and Brandon Parker were smoking pot on the baseball field. This is the sixth time Brandon has been caught on school grounds, so he's expelled for good. V just got suspended for the rest of the year."

"Holy shit," I said, slamming my locker shut. "How'd they get caught?"

"Rosemary."

"*Rosemary?* From the main office?"

"She was taking a coffee break when she saw them through a window. She snuck out the basement door and caught them red-handed."

Rosemary? Of the constant smile?

"Are you sure about this?" I asked.

Ash nodded. "Sure I'm sure. Your dad picked her up between third and fourth period. I saw him with my own two—"

I took off down the stairs and marched into the main office.

"Hi, Mara!" Rosemary sang out, her sausage bangs quivering excitedly. "How can we help you?"

"I'd like to see Mr. B."

"Well, I'm afraid he's busy right now."

I walked past her, toward Mr. B's office. As I did, her eyes narrowed but the smile was still etched onto her cheeks, making her look like an evil clown. I opened Mr. B's door without knocking, stepped inside, and closed it behind me.

Mr. B was on the phone. He glanced at me, a look of confusion on his face. Then he said some brief parting words and hung up.

"Well, this is a surprise. Would you like to sit down?"

I shook my head. "Why did you do it?"

"Why did I do what?"

"Suspend V."

Mr. B frowned. "I'm afraid that's not your business."

"Of course it's my business. V is my niece. I care what happens to her."

Mr. B swept some loose strands over his bald spot. "V broke one of our most stringent school rules."

"It's not like she was snorting cocaine," I said.

"The last time I checked," Mr. B said, "marijuana is an illegal substance. Any student who uses an illegal substance on school premises will be subjected to the appropriate disciplinary action. It's in the school handbook."

"Who wrote the handbook?"

"I did," Mr. B said. "Along with the principal and the superintendent."

"If you wrote it, why can't you change it?"

Mr. B shifted in his chair. "I'm surprised at you, Mara. You've been involved with Chemical-Free Fun Nights for years, so I would have thought—"

"I'm just saying that you have no idea what's going on in V's life right now. Maybe you should have looked into that before giving her some blind sentence."

"That's not a fair—"

"What about that parachute quote you told me, about how a mind only works when it's open? Why can't you have an open mind about—"

"Would you like a circus peanut?"

"*What?*"

Mr. B reached into the bowl on his desk and took out a few chalky orange candies, always the drudge of the Halloween bag. Popping one into his mouth, he said, "Why don't you take a seat, have a circus peanut, and calm down a little bit?"

I don't want to calm down! I thought. Without another word, I opened his door, stormed past Rosemary, and sprinted all the way out to my car.

As I was driving home, I thought about how everything feels like such a sham. Mr. B and all his comments about open minds and second chances. Rosemary's overly friendly veneer but eagerness to bust kids the first chance she gets. How I still got straight A's even when I handed in crappy work. How the only thing seniors have been talking about is whether they can smuggle alcohol into Chemical-Free Grad Night. *And circus peanuts?* How could I have ever trusted someone who eats circus peanuts?

My mom's car was in the driveway, but only halfway, like she sped back from Rochester and slammed into park as soon as she neared our house.

I pulled up behind her and headed in the side door. My parents were sitting on either end of the couch. V was sandwiched between them, hugging her knees and rocking back and forth.

They all looked up when I walked in.

"We're having an emergency Family Meeting," my dad said, frowning. "I'm not sure if you—"

"I know what happened," I said.

V stared down at her bare feet.

"We're talking to V about enrolling her in the Park Ridge Chemical Dependency teen program," my mom said.

"But I'm not a drug addict!" V cried.

"V," my dad said, "you admitted to us that this wasn't the first time . . ."

"But everyone in high school smokes pot," V said. "It's not that big of a deal."

"It was a big enough deal for you to get suspended," my dad said. "And Mara doesn't use marijuana, so it couldn't be *everyone.*"

V looked like she'd been slapped. She closed her eyes

and buried her face between her knees. Her shoulders began shaking, like she was crying, but she wasn't making any sound.

"You don't know everything about me," I said after a moment. "You don't know that I dropped out of the Johns Hopkins summer program three weeks ago. And you don't know that I'm in love with James. We've been together since March."

Silence.

V glanced up, wiping her cheeks with her hands. And then, at the exact same time, my mom said, "You dropped out of Johns Hopkins?" and my dad said, "James? Who's James?"

"James McCloskey, from Common Grounds. He's twenty-two. And, yes, I'm going to stay in Brockport this summer."

My parents both looked at me like I was this uninvited stranger posing as their daughter. I could tell their brains were working a mile a minute, loading their mental rifles. All I wanted to do was bolt out to my car or lock myself in my room.

But I wasn't going to run away from this. I was going to face it, whatever the consequences. So I stood up straight and took a deep breath and waited for the firing squad to begin.

chapter twenty-one

My parents went over to the high school and had an hour-long meeting with Mr. B. In the end, it was decided that since there was only a week left of classes, I would collect V's assignments and she would do her work from home. She would be allowed to go into school and take her final exams, but Mr. B would meet her at the front door, escort her in, and then walk her out when she was done. But other than that, V was banned from school premises until September, and he wouldn't even make an exception for my graduation.

I still thought that was excessive, but V said she was okay with the arrangement. She even agreed to do the substance-abuse counseling program. She confided to me that Brandon told her it's a total joke, basically a chance for potheads to meet and greet and make new drug connections. When I asked whether she was going to take it seriously, she said she thought so, but everything felt pretty up in the air these days.

My parents had several phone conversations with Aimee, who had already left Costa Rica and was living on the orange grove. They finally decided that Aimee would fly up to Brockport in late July to see *Angels in America* and, at that point, the four of them would sit down and talk about where V should live next year. Everyone agreed that ultimately it would be V's choice.

There was minor chaos in the Valentine household after I dropped the double bomb about James and Johns Hopkins. Actually, it wasn't as bad as I'd anticipated. I'd sat down in the comfy chair across from my parents and V and explained my reasoning about the summer program, like not rushing over my first year of college and wanting to slow down and smell the roses. They sort of seemed to get it. Even so, my mom asked me three times whether backing out of Yale was next on my agenda, and I assured her every time that it wasn't.

On the James front, my mom said, "I have to admit, I'm surprised. A guy like Travis Hart just seemed so much more . . . right."

"Travis was a jerk to me."

"A jerk?" my mom asked. "Really?"

"Are you sure James McCloskey isn't . . ." My dad trailed off. "Are you sure he isn't trying to . . . take advantage of you?"

216

I had to laugh. "That would be more Travis's department."

My parents both flushed. Even the vaguest sexual reference did the trick of shutting them up.

But the next morning, as my mom and I were loading the dishwasher, she said, "Now that I've had some time to think, it doesn't seem so surprising. You've always been so mature. It makes sense that you'd get along with someone older."

My dad wasn't evolving quite so quickly. On Sunday afternoon, James drove over to pick me up. He knew that my parents knew and my parents knew that he knew, so when he pulled into the driveway, my dad walked over and they shook hands and exchanged a few polite words.

Later, when I got home, I said to my dad, "See . . . James isn't so scary, after all?"

All my dad said was, *"Hmmph."*

"You have to admit he's nice."

"He has nice teeth."

I cracked up. "Nice teeth? Like a horse?"

"Mara, this isn't cute. I'm worried about you. I'm worried about what will happen if—"

"If you let go of your grasp on me and allow me to become my own person?"

My dad stared unblinkingly at me. I decided that now was not the right time to tell him that James and I were planning to go camping in late July, maybe over my birthday weekend.

Graduation was looming around my head like a swarm of mosquitoes. I'd finally written my speech, a two-page, double-spaced piece of crap filled with clichés. I just couldn't muster the enthusiasm to do anything better. But it was so pathetic that I made James tear up the graduation ticket I'd given him and swear he wouldn't set foot in the gym on Friday morning.

The *Brockport Post* sent a reporter over to the house to interview me about being valedictorian. We sat on Adirondack chairs in the backyard. Me, the reporter, my mom, and my dad. V was at the picnic table on the other side of the yard, hunched over a textbook. She'd been studying obsessively for finals. I'd barely even cracked a notebook.

"How does it feel to be graduating first in your class?" the reporter asked me. He had a gap between his front teeth and an Adam's apple that journeyed up and down like an elevator.

I looked over at the neighbor's cat, pressed low against the grass, inching toward his invisible prey at a painstakingly slow pace.

"It feels exhilarating," my dad said after a moment.

"All her hard work has really paid off," my mom added.

"Can I quote you on that?" the reporter asked.

"Oh, yes, of course," my mom said.

As my dad gave him the spelling of both of their names, I watched the cat take off at full speed, only to halt, baffled and empty-mouthed a few feet away.

On Wednesday afternoon, as I was walking out of my last final, Travis caught up with me. "Was that first essay a cakewalk or what? It was so obvious, I couldn't believe it. How do you think you did?"

"Are you serious?"

Travis smiled. "Come on, Valentine, tell me how you did."

"It doesn't even matter anymore."

"For old time's sake?"

"I don't want to," I said, walking faster.

We headed out the side door, toward the student parking lot. It was glaringly hot, one of those energy-draining afternoons, but I wasn't about to slow down.

"Come *on,*" Travis said. "Just tell me how you did."

I reached into my bag for my sunglasses. "Will you *stop* asking me that?"

"You know, you're a real bitch sometimes."

"Well, you're a real asshole *all* the time."

"Whoa!" Travis threw up his hands in that universal gesture of innocence. "What's your problem?"

"I don't want to play that stupid grade game anymore."

"Oh, you mean just because you kicked my ass for valedictorian, you're too good for me now?"

"It's not about that," I said as I unlocked my car door.

"Yeah, right. You won. Game over. Just admit it, Valentine. If I beat you, I'd probably do the same thing."

I didn't even answer him. I closed the door, waved goodbye, and drove over to Common Grounds. James wasn't there, but he'd left a note with the girl working the afternoon shift, saying he'd put a tall plastic cup of Famous McCloskey Chamomint Iced Tea in the fridge for me. I found it, poked a straw into the top, and crossed the street to Lift Bridge Book Shop.

I was browsing in new fiction, looking for some summer reading, when a familiar voice said, "Hey, Mara."

I glanced up. Claudia had chopped off most of her hair, and the inch or two that remained was dyed platinum blond with reddish stripes.

"Didn't recognize me?" she asked smiling.

"No . . . I'm just . . . You look great."

"Thanks."

I was about to issue the apology I'd been preparing in my head for so many months when Claudia said, "Can I talk first?"

"Sure."

"I just want to say I'm sorry."

"*You're* sorry? I'm the one who owes *you* an apology. That's what I've been wanting to tell you, but Pauline—"

Claudia shook her head. "I wasn't ready to hear it. And I definitely wasn't ready to deal with the fact that I owed you an apology, too." Claudia ran her fingers through her coppery spikes. "This is hard for me to say, but I sensed the chemistry between you and James for a long time. I kept thinking if I tried hard enough, it would go away and he'd like me instead. But that's not fair to you or James or even to me."

My throat was feeling tight. "I still shouldn't have gone behind your back."

"It's not like I gave you any other choice."

Neither of us said anything for a second.

"Aren't you wondering why I'm still in Brockport?" Claudia asked. "The college let out over a month ago."

I nodded. The plastic cup of tea was dripping with perspiration, so I wiped my fingers on my skirt.

"I'm staying here all summer," Claudia said. "I'm living with my boyfriend on Union Street."

"Boyfriend?"

Claudia smiled. "His name is Lee. He's into existential philosophy. I don't know what he's talking about half the time, but he likes me back, so that's the most important thing. And you're going to love this . . . Guess how we met?"

"How?"

"The Internet!"

"Really?"

"Brand-new redhead seeks available man to glue together her broken heart. Must have a generous bottle of Elmer's and no one else you're interested in."

My eyes were tearing up. "I'm really happy for you."

"So . . . are you and James still together?"

I nodded and looked down at my sandals.

Claudia traced her finger along the spine of a book. "This is hard for me to say . . . but I'm happy for you, too."

I started crying. Claudia began crying, too. We both just stood there, smiling and crying and shaking our heads.

Finally, Claudia wiped her eyes. "Former Common Grounds employee seeks current Common Grounds employee for hanging out this summer."

My mouth was dry, so I sipped some iced tea before saying, "I like walking on sandy beaches, eating candlelit dinners, and renewing friendships that almost fell apart."

"Me, too," Claudia said quietly.

And then we both started bawling again.

chapter twenty-two

Graduation was scheduled for Friday morning at nine. I set my alarm for seven. When it went off, I could hear my parents chatting and listening to the weather report. But a few minutes later, as I stumbled into the kitchen, they were nowhere in sight. I poured myself a glass of orange juice and sat on the tall stool. That's when I noticed the note on the cutting board.

> Mara & V -
> We drove up to Wegmans to get some muffins and fruit. Will be back in a few!
> Love,
> Mom/G-ma

I set my glass in the sink and headed upstairs to V's room. Her door was open, but she was wrapped like a dumpling in her sheet.

"Wake up!" I yanked at the blinds so light flooded into her room.

V rolled over and looked at me, a comatose expression on her face.

"Come on," I said. "Wake up . . . quick!"

"What's going on?"

"I need you to come with me."

"Where?"

"For a drive. *Come on!* We don't have a lot of time."

V wriggled out of her sheet and wobbled a little as she stood up. She was wearing an oversize T-shirt. She reached down to the floor, picked up a discarded pair of boxer shorts, and pulled them on.

"Great," I said. "Let's go."

"You're just going to wear that?"

I glanced at my old terrycloth nightgown. The straps have stretched over time, and it's hemmed for someone considerably shorter than me.

"Here." V scooped up a tank top and a pair of cut-offs. "Put these on."

V turned away as I zipped the shorts. Then I tossed the nightgown on her bed and pulled the tank top over my head. It was the hot pink one that proclaims I'M JUST A GIRL WHO CAIN'T SAY NO, but I didn't have time for a wardrobe change. We had to scram before my parents got home.

We ran down the stairs and I grabbed my car keys off

the top of the microwave. Out of habit, I shoved my cell phone and my driver's license into my front pocket.

V looked like she was still in dreamland as I pulled away from the house and turned onto Chappell Street. But once we'd driven over the canal, she rubbed her eyes and said, "Where are we going?"

"I don't know. A drive. A long drive."

"Aren't you supposed to be at graduation soon?"

I shook my head. "I'm not going."

V rotated her entire body toward me. "You're joking, right? You can't *not* go."

We passed a gas station. There was a sign out front that said CONGRATS, GRADUATES!

"Is it because of me?" V asked.

"It's because of a lot of things."

"I broke a school rule. I got in trouble. You shouldn't skip graduation because of that."

I didn't respond. V settled back into her seat. As we drove farther out of Brockport, the manicured front lawns gave way to cabbage fields. My cell phone rang. I pulled it out of my pocket and glanced down. My dad. I pushed the "cancel" button and stuffed it back in my pocket.

I drove until we reached Hamlin Beach State Park. There wasn't anyone collecting money at the gate, so I headed through and pulled into the nearest parking lot. V and I got out of the car and walked toward Lake Ontario. We were both barefoot, so we stepped carefully around

225

some shattered glass. My cell phone rang again. This time it was my mom. I didn't answer.

V and I stood next to each other, facing the immense body of grayish blue water. It was so vast I almost felt like it was surrounding me, like I was part of it. I thought about a quote I came across as I was attempting to write my valedictory address, something about how in order to discover foreign lands, you have to get lost at sea for a long time.

My cell phone rang. My dad this time. It stopped ringing. And then, just as I was about to put it back in my pocket, he tried again.

I stretched my arm behind me and threw my phone about thirty feet out. It was still ringing as it landed with a splash and disappeared beneath the water.

V giggled nervously. "Okay . . . did you really just do that?"

I waved bye-bye to the water.

"Maybe another day," V said, "we could come out here and I could throw in my . . . you know . . . my smoking stuff."

"Really?"

"I think I'm ready."

As we stared out at the water, I thought about how I've come to love V in a way that's not just obligatory family love. I can tell she feels that way about me, too. I've never told her about my conversation with Mr. B. Just like how she's never told me that she stood up for me to Dr. Hendrick. But it doesn't matter. I'm learning that

not everything has to be verbalized and analyzed and cat-
egorized.

"Are you really sure you don't want to go to graduation?" V asked.

I shrugged. "I just feel like it's all for show. For someone else's show. Like it's to make my parents happy and to
make Mr. B happy and to prove I'm better than Travis. I
don't even factor into the equation."

"Of course you do," V said. "You've earned this. You've
worked hard and you've done an amazing job. So maybe
your parents are happy. Okay, so maybe they're elated. But
Mr. B and Travis are just morons. They don't matter in
the end. This is *your* show, Mara. You've earned this day."

I flicked at a pebble with my toe. "There's not enough
time to get there anyway. I'd have to go home, take a
shower, put on my graduation dress—"

"What time did your phone say before you . . ." V pantomimed flinging it into the water.

"Eight-twenty-three."

"Let's say it's almost eight-thirty. How long would it
take to make it to the high school?"

"Twenty-five minutes. Twenty minutes if I drove fast."

"So you could get to the ceremony just in time."

"But my hair's a mess and I'm barefoot and I'm wearing your *cain't-say-no* tank top. And how can I show up at
graduation without a cap and gown?"

"You're valedictorian. You don't need a cap and gown
to tell anyone that."

"I don't even have a bra on."

"You don't—"

"No need to ram *that* point home," I said, laughing. "What about my speech? I don't have my speech with me."

"You hate your speech. You said so last night. Why don't you just wing it . . . say what's on your mind?"

"What about my parents? They won't know to come over to the high school."

"Are you kidding? I bet you *anything* they'll be there, hoping for the best. And, besides, you'll have to drop me off before you reach school premises, so I'll walk home and make double-sure they know."

"You're serious, aren't you? You really think I should do this?"

"Yeah, I really think you should."

"Well," I said. "I guess I *cain't* say no."

V cracked up. I glanced at the lake one more time. And then we hurried back to the car on the balls of our feet, careful to avoid any glass or sharp rocks.

As I screeched out of the parking lot, V screamed, "Yahooooooo!"

I laughed and rolled down my window and gunned it back to Brockport.

Also by CAROLYN MACKLER

Hardcover ISBN 0-7636-1958-2
Paperback ISBN 0-7636-2091-2

Winner of a Michael L. Printz Honor
for Excellence in Young Adult Literature

An American Library Association
Best Book for Young Adults

A Young Adult Library Services Association
Teens' Top Ten Title

A New York Public Library
Book for the Teen Age

A Michigan Library Association
Thumbs Up! Honor Title

A Pennsylvania School Librarians Association
Young Adult Top Forty Title

"Body image problems, family discord, a teenage contrarian narrating — is this anything new? Yes, because fifteen-year-old Virginia Shreves is so well-constructed a character that we like spending time with her." — *Chicago Tribune*

"Mackler writes with such insight and humor that many readers will immediately identify with Virginia's longings as well as her fear and loathing." — *Booklist*

"Mackler does a fine job introducing girls to a very cool chick with a little meat on her bones." — *The Horn Book*

"The heroine's transformation into someone who finds her own style and speaks her own mind is believable — and worthy of applause." — *Publishers Weekly*

"Carolyn Mackler writes with a clarity and impact that lifts her material above the ordinary. The book is knowing about the relationship between image and self-image, and there's genuine understanding and a welcome absence of condescension."
        — *Bulletin of the Center for Children's Books*

"Readers will be rooting for Virginia all the way as she moves from isolated TV-watcher to website-creator with purple hair and an eyebrow-ring. . . . An easy read with substance and spirit." — *Kirkus Reviews*